D1489941

Amy—

HANDLING HAVEN
(SPECIAL FORCES:
OPERATION ALPHA)

SAMANTHA A. COLE

May all your dreams come true!

S Cole

This book is a work of fiction. Names, characters, places, and incidents are products of the author's imagination or used fictitiously. Any resemblance to actual events or locales or persons living or dead is entirely coincidental.

© 2018 ACES PRESS, LLC. ALL RIGHTS RESERVED

No part of this work may be used, stored, reproduced or transmitted without written permission from the publisher except for brief quotations for review purposes as permitted by law. This book is licensed for your personal enjoyment only. This book may not be re-sold or given away to other people. If you would like to share this book with another person, please purchase an additional copy for each recipient. If you're reading this book and did not purchase it, or it was not purchased for your use only, please purchase your own copy.

Cover designed by Judi Perkins of Concierge Literary Design
Editing by Eve Arroyo

Dear Readers,

Welcome to the Special Forces: Operation Alpha Fan-Fiction world!

If you are new to this amazing world, in a nutshell the author wrote a story using one or more of my characters in it. Sometimes that character has a major role in the story, and other times they are only mentioned briefly. This is perfectly legal and allowable because they are going through Aces Press to publish the story.

This book is entirely the work of the author who wrote it. While I might have assisted with brainstorming and other ideas about which of my characters to use, I didn't have any part in the process or writing or editing the story.

I'm proud and excited that so many authors loved my characters enough that they wanted to write them into their own story. Thank you for supporting them, and me!

READ ON!
Xoxo
Susan Stoker

To Susan Stoker: Thank you for letting me be a part of your amazing and crazy world!

ABOUT THE BOOK

This book was previously published in Amazon Kindle Worlds

Haven Caldwell had the world at her feet. Traveling around the globe, hobnobbing with the elite, she did things other people could only dream of, but it was all a cover. As a covert operative of Deimos, a US black-ops agency that has more secrets than the CIA, she knew how to handle herself in any given situation, even if it required killing someone. But when her latest mission goes awry, leaving her in a wheelchair, she feels she has nothing left to live for.

Delta Force member, Sergeant First Class Lucas "Frisco" Ingram, will never forget the day he met the pretty spy whose life was turned upside down in a split second. Torn and bleeding, she begged him to leave her to die, but he couldn't do it. Now he can't get her out of his head, and she wants nothing to do with him. But when a terrorist threatens an attack on

American soil, Haven might be the only one who can help him and his teammates stop it.

While forced to work together, can Lucas convince Haven his feelings for her are not a result of guilt or pity and he has truly fallen for her? Will Haven figure out she has something worth fighting for staring her right in the face? Or will their chance for a happy-ever-after be blown to hell?

In addition to being part of Susan Stoker's Special Forces: Operation Alpha Kindle World, Handling Haven is Book 1 in the Deimos series, which is a spinoff of Samantha A. Cole's popular Trident Security series.

Deimos

Deimos—the Greek god of terror; symbolized by the serpent; son of Ares, the god of war, and Aphrodite, the goddess of beauty and love; twin brother of Phobos, the god of fear.

The United States fought for their independence, hundreds of years ago, and won. Now, they are faced with a new fight—the one against terrorism. The government has called forth operatives, hand-picked for their skills and intelligence, to defend America's borders and shield its citizens from those who wish them harm. These men and women have willingly "died" for their country, only to be reborn under a new identity, with one common goal—to hunt, and terminate, if necessary, those hell-bent on destroying the American way of life. Joining forces with elite members of the US military, they rain terror down on their adversaries whose agendas include murdering any innocents disagreeing with their religious or political beliefs.

Enemies of the United States, there is no safe place for you to hide—Deimos will find you.

CHAPTER 1

SCANNING THE CROWDED BALLROOM FILLED WITH A majority of the eight-hundred people attending the celebration, US Army Captain Keane "Ghost" Bryson studied each person diligently, trying to narrow down possible targets. Someone, or more than one someone, was not here to rub elbows with everyone else. Nope, they had an ulterior motive . . . a nefarious one. The guest list was a who's who of the famous and infamous of the world—movie stars, politicians, royalty, Fortune 500 business owners, and those who were known just because the tabloids pasted their pictures on the cover every freaking week for some stupid reason.

The festivities were for the wedding of Bollywood movie stars Vinod Kayal and Anya Nambisan. In addition to being the highest paid and most adored actress in India, Anya was also the daughter of India's Prime Minister. But word on the Dark Web, a communication and trade network for illegal transactions, was that someone was using the event to finalize a deal. Ghost and his Delta Force teammates were there to stop the sale and transfer of nuclear launch codes, under the guise of being Wesley Sutton's security team. The Virginia senator's wife, Hollywood starlet, Darby Scott, was a good friend of the bride. The couple had agreed to supply the elite soldiers with a cover since Sutton was on the senate's Homeland Security and Governmental Affairs committee. The man had proven in the past he could be trusted with the real reason for his bodyguards' presence.

Prior to the event, the team had been able to identify the seller, but the buyer, who was currently in possession of the nuke, was a mystery that hadn't been solved yet. Ghost's head was on constant swivel as he mentally assessed and cataloged everyone in sight. There were a few other undercover Delta Team members scattered about the grand ballroom, as well as outside on the huge patio and manicured lawn, where some people were enjoying the pleasant evening air. The rest of the highly-trained team were hidden in the thick jungle surrounding the venue's compound, a few miles outside Mumbai's city limits.

His gaze passed over a small group of guests conversing before zipping back to them as recognition kicked in. While he didn't know the dark-haired beauty in a stunning, blue evening gown, her tuxedoed date was all too familiar to the Delta Force soldier. He stood a commanding six foot four, his long, dirty-blond hair pulled back in a ponytail at his nape, and could kill someone in at least two dozen ways. The man with one name worked for Deimos, an American black-ops agency that ninety-nine percent of the population didn't know existed.

"Fuck," Ghost whispered, catching the attention of his teammate standing next to him, also wearing a monkey suit. Damn, he hated undercover gigs that required black tie attire. The noose around his neck was practically strangling him.

Being the trained operative he was, Cormac "Fletch" Fletcher remained stoic and seemingly unaffected by the muttered curse. "What's up?"

"Your ten o'clock."

Turning slowly, Fletch zeroed in on the problem. "Well, shit. What the fuck is Carter doing here?"

"I don't know, but I can guarantee he's not just

here for the food." Once, just once, Ghost wished the US government and military branches would talk to each other and share a few secrets so their operatives weren't shocked and pissed when they found out someone else was most likely undercover for the same damn reasons.

As if he felt their eyes upon him, the spy looked in their direction while laughing at something that was said in the group. His gaze met Ghost's for only a split second, but there was no doubt he'd recognized the two Deltas who he'd run into on undercover missions before. Hopefully, he was using the alias they knew about—the CEO of a very successful import/export company. While the business was legitimate, it was really run by Deimos to supply their operatives with a cover that was nearly impenetrable.

With his arm around his date, Carter strolled away from the group, and, without looking at them, slowly meandered his way over to where Ghost and Fletch were standing on the outskirts of the crowd. The couple chatted as they moved, giving the appearance they were just like every other guest in the room—who wasn't a spy or terrorist. Thankfully, Carter was one of the good guys and worked for the

US of A, because what little Ghost knew of him, he could earn a similar eerie moniker like Phantom, Phantasm, or Shadow. The spy could float in and back out of any situation, and if he didn't want you to know he was there, you never would.

The couple had almost passed right by them, when Carter feigned a double take, snapped his fingers, and pointed at Ghost. "Hey, John Benbrook, right? You were on my security team a few years ago. Either that or you could be his twin."

John Benbrook was one of Ghost's aliases and the one he'd used several times in the other man's presence. And since he'd been standing here, pretending to be a bodyguard, it was the best way to start the conversation the spy apparently wanted to have. Also in those three brief sentences, he'd given Ghost enough information to hold up his side of the dialogue. While his real name was T. Carter—no one knew what the T stood for, or if they did they weren't telling or still alive—the persona he'd cultivated over the years was Carter Burke.

"Yes, sir, Mr. Burke. Nice to see you again." He extended his hand for the other man to shake.

"It's been a while, but I never forget a face or a name. Darling, this is John Benbrook. He was on my

5

security team before moving onto bigger fish. John, this is my girlfriend and associate, Jordyn Dominguez." In other words, the gorgeous woman was also here in an undercover capacity. It was a fair bet her surname was an alias, but it was up for grabs on whether her first name was real. Some agents found it easier to alter one instead of both.

Ghost dipped his chin once. "Pleased to meet you, Ms. Dominguez." He gestured to Fletch. "Allow me to introduce you to my teammate, Keith Shelton." Carter knew Fletch's real name, but the alias was a new one. The two men shook hands as he explained, "We're on Senator Sutton's detail tonight, although, I miss the days covering your back. Skydiving and racing Lamborghinis is a lot more fun than watching everyone else get drunk and try to top each other with how much money they have. And don't even get me started on the politics."

The spy snorted. "Anytime you want to join me again, you're more than welcome. But I'm actually a little surprised you're here. A mutual friend of ours and his buddies are camping in the woods this weekend, and I could have sworn he told me you and a few guys were going too."

Oh, shit. He raised his eyebrows in mild curiosity at the man's veiled statement—anyone eavesdropping wouldn't have a clue the man was talking about anything but camping—however on the inside, Ghost's stomach plummeted as his heart rate sped up. *Potential Clusterfuck-101, here we come.*

"WHY THE FUCK ARE THEY TALKING ABOUT CAMPING?" Lucas "Frisco" Ingram asked his temporary teammate, Graham "Hollywood" Caverly. They were lying on the ground, under the cover of the jungle, with their weapons and binoculars pointed at the compound, an hour or so before sunset. Frisco and a few others from his squad, Trigger, Lefty, Oz, and Grover, were with the other man's team for a joint mission in India. They'd already been outside the venue for hours and had a few more to go before the festivities wound down. With any luck, though, the exchange would happen soon and team members inside got what they needed—the launch codes and the person who had possession of the nuke.

Before Hollywood, or anyone else listening through their comm units, could answer him, the soft crack of a twig behind them had Frisco flipping over, his weapon up, ready to fire. He stared in disbelief at the grinning, camouflaged man leaning against a tree, with his empty hands in full view to show he wasn't about to shoot them in the back. It took a moment for Frisco to realize Hollywood hadn't had the same response to the person who'd snuck up on them. He was still surveying the compound as if he'd expected someone to show up out of the blue. "If you just got me killed, dude, my wife's going to rip you a new one."

"She should rip him a new one just for the hell of it." Behind his face paint, the newcomer's smile grew wider. "Mind if I join you twatwaffles?"

"As I was about to say, before we were so rudely interrupted . . ." Hollywood continued, ignoring the man's question, ". . . the 'camping' references were to let us know we're not the only ones in this damn jungle. Sawyer, what the hell are you and your frogs doing here?"

Pushing off the tree, the man dropped to the ground and crawled forward to take the spot on Hollywood's left. Relieved there was no threat, Frisco returned to his original position on his stomach to his teammate's right.

"Probably the same thing you're doing here . . . except I'm getting paid a helluva lot more than you. Thank God for the private sector. And you'll be happy to know I've hired more people, and they're not all Navy. Never let it be said I'm not impartial to the lesser branches of the military. Who's he?"

Hollywood's eyes remained glued to his binoculars as he made the introductions. "Ian Sawyer, retired SEAL and sarcastic son of a bitch. Lucas Ingram, current Delta and twatwaffle. I like that . . . I'm gonna have to use that."

"Nope. I've got the copyright on it. Come up with your own damn insult. In fact, I've been using that for someone else, lately. I'll have to think of a new one for this mission. Hmm. Taint-waffle . . . still rolls smoothly off my tongue. I like it." Sawyer settled in and pulled out his own binoculars. "Now that that's taken care of . . . since we're probably here for the same damn reason, what frequency are you boys on, so we're not stepping on each other's toes out here?"

Activating the microphone on his comms unit, Hollywood said, "Hey, Ghost, we got a couple of Trident frogs who want in on our frequency. You okay with that?"

A single *click* was his answer.

"Did Daddy say we're allowed to join your sweet-sixteen party or is he worried we'll spike the punch?" Sawyer snarked as he surveyed the crowd on the patio.

Between the man's name and the mention of

Trident, Frisco now knew who they were dealing with. The world of black ops was a relatively small one in the grand scheme of things, and even if you were meeting someone from it for the first time, you'd probably already heard about them from other members of the community. Ian Sawyer and his brother Devon had retired from SEAL Team Four a few years ago and started Trident Security in Tampa, Florida. The company took on cases from the private sector and government contracts, specifically from the FBI, CIA, and Deimos. That last agency was still a large enigma in that, until just recently, a scant few people had known it even existed and that included members of the black-ops community.

"Yup, you're in. But you owe him a case of scotch ... the good stuff."

Frisco grinned for the first time since the other man had snuck up on them, knowing Ghost had said no such thing.

After Hollywood rattled off the frequency the team was currently using, Sawyer repeated the info to someone named "Polo" over his own unit. Within seconds, there were several clicks and then the two groups were suddenly able to communicate with each other. Frisco took over the watch as the two men to his left compared maps of the surrounding area and alerted their own team members about who was within shooting distance so no one got caught up in friendly fire. It was bad enough they had to worry about the armed guards patrolling the outer edges of the compound spotting them.

"Damn, I wish these two fuckers would just meet up already," Frisco grumbled about twenty minutes later, after all was quiet over the comms once more, except the chatter from the party inside. "Then we can take them both out and get the hell out of here with the codes and nuke."

Sawyer yanked the binoculars from his eyes and glared at Hollywood and Frisco. "What do you mean take *both* of them out? Damn it, this is what fucking happens when those dingleberries back in Washington don't talk to each other." He activated his microphone again. "Hey, Jackass, Sweetheart, and Vixen, there's a price on your boy's head. Ghost, under no circumstances do any of your men shoot the guy with the damn codes. He's friendly."

Hollywood groaned. "Are you fucking kidding me? He's a plant?"

"More like a dweeb, but yeah, we need to get him out in one piece."

For the next thirty seconds or so, there was back

and forth conversation between Ghost, Fletch, Carter, and the woman, Jordyn, about some guy who worked for an import/export company. It was all fictional, of course. The end result was they were all on the same page—finally. "Preston Ward" was now off the Deltas' hit list. Unfortunately, the one person who remained on it was still an unknown entity.

Once he was satisfied their inside man was not going to end up in the morgue, Sawyer gave the Deltas a quick intel report. "The dweeb is from Deimos—one of their support guys using a cover that's been cultivated for years. His date, Vixen, is an operative. Egghead, get with whomever Delta's got on the wires and send out the pic of Reardon and Caldwell. They get extracted no matter what; resistance isn't in the dweeb's vocabulary. He won't last sixty seconds."

Great, just great. That meant the guy wasn't trained in SERE—Survival, Evasion, Resistance, and Escape. If he was captured and tortured, he'd be spilling his guts in no time. Not what you wanted to hear about a black-ops agent, even if he was on the support team. He still probably knew enough to cause huge problems for Deimos and the President of the United States.

A few seconds after Beckett "Coach" Ralston and

Sawyer's man synchronized their databases, Frisco's miniature tablet vibrated in his pocket, and he pulled it out. When a photo of a couple popped up, he studied it. They were dressed in formal wear—a tuxedo on the red-haired guy, while the looker wore a gold evening gown with a thigh-high slit in the skirt. And damn, was she hot. Her chestnut-colored hair was down and full of curls that framed her heart-shaped face. Without knowing how tall the guy was, and with nothing else in the photo to use in comparison, it was difficult to tell how tall she was. But with that mile-long leg that was exposed, Frisco figured she was somewhere between five seven and five nine, which was three to five inches shorter than he was. While she had curves, it was obvious to him she was in excellent physical condition, which was in direct contrast to her "date," whose arm was around her waist as they grinned for the camera. It was evident they knew each other well, and an odd jolt of jealousy struck Frisco as he assessed the other man. The lucky bastard looked like he spent most of his time indoors behind a computer—he was pale, skinny with almost no muscle tone, and his black-rimmed glasses had "nerd" written all over them—not that there was anything wrong with that. The "nerds" and "geeks" of this world held a lot more power than most gave them credit for. Hell, Coach's wife, Harley, was a computer geek . . . and she was pretty damn hot, too.

"Coach, are you fucking with the damn feeds?" the guy named "Egghead" queried in a pissed-off tone.

"Nope—was just going to ask you the same thing. I've got garbage on half of them."

"What's wrong?" Sawyer and Hollywood spoke into their comms at the same time.

Sawyer's man was the first to reply, "We've got some sort of interference on a few of the feeds— they're coming in as static, and I don't think it's random. Someone else is hacked in besides the two of us."

"Fuck," his boss replied. "Who else wants to throw a monkey wrench into this gig? Find out where it's coming from and make it fast. I've got a bad feeling about this."

Before anyone could respond, that bad feeling Frisco and all the other operatives were now experiencing became reality when an explosion rocked the compound, followed by screams and all hell breaking loose. A ball of flames blew out several windows, spraying everyone standing on the patio with shattered glass, sending them running for cover.

A chorus of curses came over the comm units. Murphy's law just went FUBAR again. The mission was officially fucked up beyond all recognition. *Shit.*

CHAPTER 2

HAVEN CALDWELL SQUEEZED HER "DATE'S" ARM. "You're doing fine, Preston," she assured him in a low voice, using the name of the reclusive computer developer he was pretending to be. "Just relax."

"Easy for you to say," Kenny Reardon responded, while tugging on the collar of his tuxedo and the black tie encircling it. He was only two years her junior, but his pale, baby face, covered in freckles, made him appear far younger than that. "You don't have a target on your back."

She cupped his chin and turned his head so he was looking directly at her. To anyone else in the room, it probably seemed like she was seducing the socially-handicapped but rich man. However, in reality, they were just friends. She'd known Kenny for about eight years, ever since he'd been hired as one of the analysts at Deimos, five years after she'd been trained to be one of their operatives at the age of twenty-one. He'd been assigned as the intelligence and communications contact for her and several other agents and, over the years, had become like a kid brother to her. They spoke almost daily, and when she was in town, they occasionally went out to dinner or to a movie. Some of the few times Haven was able to let down her hair and be herself—unfortunately, she had no idea who that person was anymore.

Some of the support staff and agents at the covert organization's headquarters in California had become a close-knit family, considering most of them had been employed based on the fact they didn't have any. Few people in the world even knew Deimos existed—the CIA was a Boy Scout troop compared to it—and those who did, knew to keep their mouths shut. Haven and her fellow operatives did the President's and US government's dirty work —not that anyone in power would admit it. They took care of things, which the public could never know about, to keep the US safe from terrorists and other world powers who wanted to see the leader of the free world fall flat on its face. Deimos was the

Greek god of terror, so it was the ideal name for the black-ops agency that excelled in torture and assassinations, among other things.

For years, Haven had traveled all over the world, using various aliases. Sometimes, like this evening, she hobnobbed with the elite, while on other missions, she could be in one of the worst hellholes on Earth. It wasn't hard to figure out which assignments she preferred. But this was Kenny's first time, and most likely his last, in the field. They'd needed the super geek for his extensive computer knowledge, specifically about the Dark Web, in the event the operative was tested. "Preston Ward" was one of hundreds of profiles the agency had spent years updating for times just like this. There were few photos of the fictional man on the internet, all of which were hazy or taken from the back, and several members of the Deimos support staff could actually pass as "Preston" whenever the time came to use the profile. Reardon had just happened to draw the short straw, and it was Haven's job to make sure he got out of the mission in one piece.

"Hey, you know I won't let anything happen to you. Just stick to me like glue, hot stuff."

"Well, at least that's not a hardship. I've got the hottest looking date here tonight."

Haven grinned. When she'd first gotten to know Reardon, a simple exchange like that would have had his cheeks and neck turning beet red as he stuttered through a response. Even now, if a woman he barely knew just smiled at him, he would still have the same reaction. But over time, he'd gotten comfortable with the female agents such as Haven and Jordyn Alvarez. Sometimes they liked to tease him, but usually they preferred to build up his self-assurance around women. He was a sweet kid, and she would love for some lucky girl to realize that someday. In fact, not too long ago, while Carter was away on a solo mission, Haven and Jordyn had been at headquarters for some new training and had taken Kenny out to a bar for dinner after his shift had ended one night. Both women were used to being hit on in most social settings, and that night had been no exception. However, they'd given all their attention to their friend, making him feel ten feet tall and bulletproof. She was sure the other women in the bar that night had been wondering what was so special about him that had Haven and Jordyn ignoring every other man in the place. Kenny would probably always be shy around women he didn't know, but, hopefully, they'd given him the confidence to get past that so he could talk to one he was interested in without getting tongue tied.

Hooking her arm around his elbow, Haven gestured to the main doors to the ballroom. "Let's take a walk through the rest of the place. Hopefully, we'll run into 'Mr. Smith' soon."

Mr. Smith, undoubtedly not his real name, had popped up on the Dark Web a few months ago. The Dark Web was the side of the internet most people didn't know was a reality and not just something they read about in a spy novel. Smith had been trolling for anyone who might have a specific software protection dongle with launch codes for a suitcase-sized nuclear device. It was one of many that'd gone missing from Russia back in the 1990s. Using the Preston Ward profile, the agents at Deimos headquarters had begun laying an intricate trail about how the developer/hacker had come into possession of the codes. They were then contacted by Smith who wanted to purchase the codes for the tidy sum of $10 million. After providing "proof" Preston had the codes, the agents had then engaged in a game of cat and mouse which was hopefully coming to an end tonight. Once they identified who Smith really was, he'd be quietly taken into custody by Deimos agents, who would then stop at nothing to recover the device.

Haven sashayed toward the open double doors leading into a foyer that was larger than most high-end hotel suites she'd been in. The long skirt of the shiny, gold Badgley Mischka dress she wore swished from side to side as she moved. An above-the-knee slit exposed her left leg with each step, without showing the small handgun strapped to her right thigh just below her crotch. Tucked below the deep V of the dress's neckline was a garrote, which she could easily access in the event she needed to silently dispatch someone by strangulation. It wasn't a method she liked to use since it meant getting up close and personal with her enemy, but it was there in case she needed it. The matching shoes also had some modifications the designer had never intended. A three-inch stiletto knife slid through a small slit just below the seat of the four-inch heels and rested along the shank under the sole. All she had to do was bend one knee, reach down, and slide the knife out from under the shoe, and she'd have instant weapon in hand. If James Bond were a woman, she'd have loved the shoes as much as Haven did.

As they strolled throughout parts of the 50,000

square feet of the ridiculously opulent venue, Haven steered Reardon into areas with less people in them, giving Mr. Smith a better opportunity to approach them. The wedding festivities were expected to continue well into the night, and she hoped it wouldn't take that long for him to contact the "code seller." Mixed in with all the wedding guests were bodyguards, the catering staff, and the event coordinator's people, but even though most of the hired help were in tuxedos, it was easy for Haven's keen eye to distinguish them—it was all in the harried or precise way they moved, depending on their job.

Passing through a room that housed a small bar and several intimate sitting areas for guests to enjoy, Haven smiled and nodded hello to several people who knew her as Hazel McPherson, "owner" of Simply Splendid, Inc., a moderate-sized, international cosmetics and skin care company that was another business Deimos used for its operatives' covers. Exiting into the hallway, she glanced to the right and then left, getting her bearings before deciding which way to go. She'd studied the floor plans of the mansion for days, making sure she knew how to get out of there if the mission went south. Other Deimos agents were among the guests and staff milling about as her backup, but Reardon was her main responsibility, and there was no way she'd let him get hurt or killed.

As she turned left down the long hall, she headed for the two-story library. This far away from the main ballroom the lively music being played there had faded away and was replaced with the soft chamber music coming from their new destination. More guests were entering another room further down on the opposite side of the hall that was designated as a cigar bar. Having thought of everything, the venue had a special ventilation system in that closed-door room for the smoke to be removed and released up through the roof, three stories above it, without exposing the rest of the rooms.

A few steps before they reached the open door of the library, Haven felt the hairs on the back of her neck stand on end, sending a tingling warning throughout her body. She surveyed her surroundings carefully. At the far end of the hallway, past the cigar bar, a tuxedoed man stood sentry, appearing as one of the guards stationed throughout the building. Glancing behind her, Haven noticed two other men in formal wear approaching, but neither gave her the impression they were part of the staff. No, they were guests—or were they? She hadn't been able to stare without drawing attention to herself, but one of the men looked familiar, and, as she guided Reardon into the library, she wracked her brain to figure out where she knew the man from. He had dark hair and a trimmed beard, which barely covered a scar on his left cheek. Slender, he stood a little over six feet tall. That's all she'd been able to catalog in her mind without a second look.

"What's wrong?" Kenny whispered. "You're frowning."

Haven was surprised he'd picked up on that considering she almost always had her game face on while undercover. But something niggled her brain about that one man. Keeping her eyes on the doorway, she leaned forward and gave Kenny a kiss near his ear. "I think I recognized someone, but I don't know where I know him from. I need a better look."

"Vixen, repeat. Didn't get that last transmission," Sawyer said in a low voice through her earpiece.

Positioning herself and her date so she could observe the unknown man if he came into or passed by the room, Haven waited. In the meantime, since two older couples were now nearby, she couldn't respond to Sawyer directly, so she let him know she was stalling while it appeared she was answering a question Kenny had asked moments earlier. "I'm not sure, honey. I'll have to check my calendar when I get a chance."

Seconds ticked by. Just when she thought he must have turned around and gone back in the other direction, an ultra-bright light flashed a split second before a deafening roar filled the air. The floor shook as books came flying off the shelves and the floor-to-ceiling windows blew out. Haven, Reardon, and other people in the room were thrown off their feet by the compression blast, along with anything that wasn't nailed down.

Oh, God! Not again!

Total chaos ensued. People were screaming or moaning, but Haven's ears were ringing so loudly she couldn't hear anything other than the blaring fire alarm. Searing smoke permeated the room, setting off the sprinkler system, which seemed woefully inadequate for the circumstances while still soaking those standing underneath the spray heads. The explosion hadn't occurred in the library, but somewhere close by—a room or two further down the hall toward the cigar bar.

Pain shot through her left arm where there was a gash from something that had hit her. She ignored it as she reached out—almost blindly as thousands of black, white, and gray dots danced before her eyes—

trying to find Reardon among the debris. Grabbing a leg, she was relieved when her blurry vision cleared enough to see it was the Deimos geek, and he was alive, although stunned. Kicking off her shoes—they'd be difficult to run in—Haven rolled to her feet, and pulled her gun from its holster, not worried her thong-covered crotch was briefly exposed. Her head was spinning as she scanned the room for any other threats.

"Get up!" she shouted to Reardon, unsure if he'd heard her since she could barely hear her own voice. She brought her hand to her ear and found the listening device, that'd been hidden by her hair, had been knocked out. Bending down, she yanked on Reardon's arm, trying to get him to understand her and get moving. He shook his head, as if trying to clear it, as he slowly got to his knees.

Glancing toward the door, Haven was horrified to see two men in respirator masks enter the room with guns in their hands. Instinctively knowing things had just turned into a kill or be killed situation—there was no way they could have outfitted themselves so quickly against the smoke unless they'd known it was coming—she raised the weapon in her right hand and fired, striking the closest man in the chest. He fell to the floor, the bullet to his heart stopping it cold. The second man reacted quickly by diving to his left when Haven shifted her aim. Her shot hit the back of the sofa he'd disappeared behind. With limited ammo, she couldn't afford to waste any, she'd have to wait for him to pop up to fire another shot. That didn't mean she was just going to stand there as an open target, though.

Not knowing if they could get out through the hallway, Haven propelled Reardon toward one of the blown-out windows as soon as he got his feet under him. It would be about an eight-foot drop. Ignoring the other injured people in the room, Haven kept her weapon aimed at the sofa as she pointed to the window. "Jump!" she ordered her charge, grateful she'd been able to hear herself through all the other noise that time. Obeying her was one thing she'd drilled into Reardon during the weeks leading up to the mission. If she gave him a command, he was to follow it without hesitation; both their lives might depend on it.

Blood was flowing from a laceration to his head, but Reardon, thankfully, didn't waste any time grabbing hold of the window frame, checking how far he had to fall, then leaping out. Firing one more shot at the sofa, Haven grabbed the skirt of her dress, then stepped through the glassless frame and jumped.

Landing, she rolled as she hit the stone patio, letting her momentum absorb most of the impact. Bits of broken glass ripped the soles of her feet and her bare arms. Paying no attention to them, she was moving forward before she was completely standing again, pushing Reardon in front of her to where the Trident boys would be waiting to cover and extract them. "Run to the trees!"

Each step was painful, but she shoved it from her mind—there'd be time to tend to her injuries later. Zigzagging through all the guests, who'd already escaped from other rooms in a panic, Reardon and Haven hit the lawn running. The crowd thinned out about halfway to the jungle. Just when she thought they were going to make it, something slammed into her back, knocking the breath from her lungs. Her feet flew out from under her as she fell forward, an involuntary scream caught in her throat. Her back was on fire, agony ripping through every nerve. Reflexively, her hands shot out to protect her from the fall, but she still landed hard. Glancing over his shoulder, Reardon saw her go down, and he slid to a stop so fast he ended up on his ass.

Pushing against her hands, Haven struggle to get back up—there was only about fifty yards to go to the safety the jungle and armed operatives would provide—but she couldn't make her feet and legs obey her brain's commands. *What the fuck?* It took a moment for it to register that she couldn't move them. Terror coursed through her as she tried to deny what she was quickly realizing—it'd been a bullet that had struck her, and her legs were now paralyzed. *Oh, God, no!*

CHAPTER 3

THE WEDDING HAD GONE FROM A CELEBRATION OF life, and the union of a publicly-adored couple, to complete and utter chaos. The explosion had occurred somewhere inside the building, sending hundreds of people running for the closest exits. They were pouring out of every door and even some windows. Frisco hadn't seen anyone come out injured, yet, but several people had fallen under the crush of the crowd. Women were crying and scream-ing; men were yelling and frantically trying to figure out what the hell was going on. Smoke began to filter out from the center of the roof as flames shot skyward.

Frisco and the others hiding in the jungle ran through the list of those inside. One by one, the voices of Ghost, Fletch, Carter, Jordyn, and several other operatives inside the mansion came over the comms. They hadn't been close enough to the blast zone to be seriously wounded, although there were some minor injuries. But others were still unaccounted for. The backup teams had yet to hear the Deimos geek and his female bodyguard report in, but with the earsplitting pandemonium going on around them, there could be any number of reasons why. There was no way of knowing if the explosion was related to the pending sale of the codes or something else altogether. Either way, it'd been totally unexpected. Unless the two main targets checked in soon, Sawyer said he was going to order his team to move in to recover them. They couldn't allow anything to happen to either of them—if they were still alive.

"Does anyone have eyes on Vixen and her boy?" the Trident team leader barked into his microphone for the third time in less than a minute, as he, Hollywood, and Frisco scanned the panicked crowd still emerging from the building. People dressed in gowns and tuxedos were pushing others out of the way, ignoring those who fell. Victims were being trampled which could be just as deadly as another bomb going off.

Sawyer received a round of "negatives" from several operatives before someone Frisco didn't know responded, "Boss-man, we've got to get those people out of there. The fire's spreading fast."

There had to be victims still inside, injured or stunned from the initial explosion, who couldn't escape on their own, and from the look of things, everyone else was trying to save their own hides. Since Trident Security was in the private sector, and the US government could deny knowing why they were there, them exposing themselves was the better option. The Delta Team, however, was comprised of active-duty Army personnel, and it would be a lot harder to explain why they were on foreign soil, covertly surrounding the compound with heavy-duty firearms. Those inside, though, could still maintain their covers and help the injured. It only took a split second for Sawyer to answer his team-mate. "Agreed, Boomer. Ghost, can your team cover our sixes and watch for the principals? We'll try to get as many of them out, but this is probably a diversion. I don't want my team caught with their pants down."

"Affirmative," Delta's team leader responded, his raspy voice a result of the smoke. "Jungle Cats, maintain . . . *cough* . . . positions and make sure the frogs are . . . *cough* . . . covered. Monkey Suits, if you can hear me, help evacuate the injured. Everyone keep your eyes open for the missing principals. Snow White and Prince Charming are on their way out with Sleepy. Grumpy, they're all yours." The senator and his wife had been briefed that if there was an emergency they were to go straight to their limousine with the closest Delta operative, where another one would be waiting to drive them to safety.

"Alpha & Omega, move in. Keep your faces covered. Jackass and Sweetheart, find the damn principals and get them out of there." Sawyer pulled on the balaclava he'd yanked out of one of the many pockets in his camo pants. While his teams had applied face paint, just as Frisco, Hollywood, and the other Deltas in the jungle had, they didn't want to be caught on camera where facial recognition software could possibly help identify them. Many of the uninjured, but stunned, wedding guests milling about the large lawn were already recording the turmoil on their cell phones. It was a fair bet the videos would be on *YouTube* within minutes.

As Sawyer stood and tucked his weapon in its holster on his right hip, a flash of gold caught Frisco's attention. There she was, the woman from the picture, materializing from the crowd with her "date," urging him to run straight toward where Frisco and the others were still hidden amidst the foliage. They were both covered in dirt, soot, and blood, and the brunette was barefoot and limping, although it didn't look like it was slowing her down much. Frisco was about to announce he had eyes on the principals, when a loud crack rang out above all the other noise—to the trained ear it was the unmistakable sound of a gun being fired. He watched in horror as the woman's back bowed from the impact, and she fell forward, her face contorting in pain.

"Shit!" Frisco was on his feet and running before she'd completely fallen onto the grass beneath her, with Hollywood and Sawyer on his heels, the latter shouting out orders to the combined team members. The redheaded kid realized the woman protecting him was down, and he skidded to a halt, his feet coming out from under him. Landing on his ass, he twisted around and began to crawl back to her. Another gun report, this one distinctly from a long-range rifle, echoed from somewhere behind and to the right of Frisco, followed by a voice coming over the comms. "Alpha Four, threat from library window eliminated." Whatever his name was, he had to be a sniper on one of Sawyer's teams.

Some of the guests realized shots were being

fired and that started everyone freaking out and ducking or diving to the ground to make themselves less of a target. Crying and sobs became screams of alarm again. No one knew where to run, so they were slamming into and tripping over each other in their fright.

Frisco dodged around several people running for the cover the trees behind him could provide. As he neared the downed couple, he swung his Colt-M4 around to his back by its strap so it was out of the way. Sliding like a baseball player trying to beat a tag at home plate, he stretched out next to the injured woman, confident the two other men had his six. They stood over them, their weapons at the ready, scanning for more threats, as he got to his knees. The female operative's wide-eyed charge had been about to roll her over, but Frisco stopped him. "Wait!" He eyed the bullet hole in the back of her dress, in the region of her midline, lumbar spine. *Shit, that's not good!* "Come over to my side and grab her legs. We'll roll her as one unit."

While the shaken geek obeyed the order, crawling over to kneel next to the woman's hips and thighs, Frisco reached across her back and grasped her opposite shoulder with one hand and her waist with the other. After making sure the other man was ready, he said, "On the count of three. One . . . two . . . three."

As they gently rolled her over, another explosion shook the ground. Screams of terror followed as the crowd started running again, this time toward the parking lot and their vehicles, which most couldn't access due to the valets having their keys. But several limousines were already barreling toward the exit and the roadway beyond. Brisk intel was reported over the comm units followed by more gunfire. Apparently, whatever was happening was on the far side of the compound, and Frisco prayed it stayed there as he stared into the wounded woman's face.

She grabbed his arm, her pretty, brown eyes and pale face were filled with pain and . . . resignation? Her voice was raspy and weak. "L-Leave me."

"Not on your life, darling. We're gonna get you out of here."

She shook her head. "No. C-Can't move my legs. Leave m-me."

Shock and anger rose within him as what she was telling him sank in. She was paralyzed and wanted him to leave her to die—to be killed by whomever was behind the attack, whether swiftly or following hours of torture. *Like fucking hell!*

As the gunfire grew louder, Sawyer snapped into

his microphone, "Babs! Get the fuck in here! West lawn—critical extraction!"

A female voice answered over the sounds of a chopper's rotor blade, "Coming in hard and fast, Boss-man."

It was nice to know someone had brought the big toys. Behind his teammate, Hollywood fired his weapon. "Get her up, Frisco! Tangos are moving in. We gotta get out of here fast!"

"I can't! She can't move her legs!"

"Pick her up! The damage is already done!" To anyone else, his teammate's words would probably sound harsh and callous. But Frisco had heard the regret in them along with the unspoken message that if they didn't get her out of there fast, things would get a lot worse—for all of them. He didn't have a choice. There was no way he was leaving her to die—no way any of them would.

A rapid thumping, signaling the approach of a helicopter, increased as did the gunfire. A Black-hawk appeared low above the treeline and, indeed, it was coming in "hard and fast." Thankfully, most of the guests had run for their lives by this point so the grassy expanse between the burning mansion and the jungle was basically clear for the pilot to land. A few stragglers quickly got out of the way, unsure if this was a new attack. Hollywood and Sawyer were both now firing their weapons at targets as several bullets hit the dirt not far from the ragtag group. All around the six-acre property, Delta, Trident, and Deimos team members were engaging the enemy that seemed to grow in numbers. It was unclear how many of them were actually just the hired security for the event, who had no idea who the good guys were and weren't, and were shooting at anyone with a weapon. Unlucky for them, there was no way to tell the difference between the tangos and the armed innocents, either.

Frisco knew they were out of time and options. Ignoring the pain and fear etched on the injured woman's face and her repeated pleas for him to leave her, he got to his feet, gestured for the geek to move out of the way, and grasped her right ankle. The maneuver he was about to do was called a Ranger Roll and one he'd practiced many times with his teammates. It was the fastest way to pick up an unconscious or incapacitated person while under fire. Dropping his right shoulder, he did a quick somersault over her left hip, bringing her lower body with him. When he rolled back onto his knees, he had her in a fireman's carry as she hung limply across his shoulders.

Sawyer reached down and grabbed the redhead by the collar of his tuxedo jacket, dragging him to his feet. "Get up and on the fucking chopper, Reardon! Move!"

Not waiting to see if the others were following, Frisco stood and ran toward the Blackhawk as it touched down less than twenty yards away, ducking low to avoid the rapidly moving rotor blades. The rear door was open, and a man, dressed in black, wearing a balaclava, covered Frisco and the others with a mounted M-60 machine gun, as they high-tailed it across the lawn. As they neared, Sawyer ran past everyone and vaulted through the open door, before turning around and holding out his hand to Frisco. The two men grasped each other's forearms, and Sawyer yanked him and the woman into the rear bay. Hollywood practically threw Reardon into the chopper before jumping in himself.

"Go, Babs! Go!" Sawyer yelled to his female pilot.

As Frisco lowered the injured operative to the floor as gently as he could, the Blackhawk lifted off the ground. Just as fast as it had landed, it was back up in the air, banking toward the treeline again. The Trident team leader yelled again, this time into the comm's microphone, "Alpha, Omega, Delta, principals secure. Ghost, Devil Dog's taking my lead down there. We've got Hollywood and whatever Taint-waffle's name is again. We're medevacing to our standby."

Kneeling next to the woman, Frisco realized she was no longer responsive. Her eyes were shut, and her head was rolled to the side. His heart leaped into his throat until he realized she was still breathing. She'd either passed out from blood loss or the pain —it didn't matter which, but it was probably better that she was out. The man who'd already been on the chopper ripped off his face mask and dragged a large medical duffel out from under the row of jump seats. He and Sawyer worked together to cut the woman's dress so they could assess her injuries. Frisco spotted a trauma blanket tucked in the duffel among the medical equipment and snatched it. Tearing open the package, he spread it out and covered her nearly naked body after they saw there was no exit wound on her chest, abdomen, or flanks. The bullet was still inside her somewhere—that could either be a good or bad thing, but one they couldn't rectify in the airborne tin can. Rolling her as one unit, the three trained operatives located the wound on her lower back. It'd matched up with the hole in her now discarded dress, right near her spine.

"Just get her stabilized, Skipper," Sawyer ordered the man who'd been posted on the helicopter, before addressing the others. "We're heading for Kearsarge."

Frisco had figured that was their initial destination. The Navy's third Wasp-class amphibious assault ship USS Kearsarge, was currently located in the Arabian Sea. The crew had been ordered to take position in international waters, offshore from Mumbai, in case Delta needed them. Apparently, it'd been arranged for Sawyer's team and Deimos to use the ship, with its advanced medical services, as well. At least someone had known there'd be more than one military branch or government agency working this mission from hell. The doctors onboard would be able to perform surgery and stabilize Haven. From there, they'd fly her out on an Osprey to an airbase where she'd be transferred onto a plane en route to Landstuhl Regional Medical Center, the US military hospital in Germany—if she survived until then. Frisco's heart clenched at the thought.

Hollywood poured Quikclot powder onto the wound, slowing the blood flow, then placed a trauma dressing over it, before they rolled her onto her back again. Skipper started an IV in her left arm. There was nothing else any of them could do until they reached the ship except remove as many slivers of glass as they could from her feet and arms and clean the wounds. Reardon sat on the edge of one of the jump seats, unashamed tears rolling down his face as he held the unconscious woman's hand as she lay at his feet. The worry in his voice was clear as he yelled to her over the sounds of the rotors slicing through the air. "Haven, you're gonna be okay. You hear me, Haven? You're gonna be okay."

Unwilling to sever the connection he'd begun to feel toward her the moment he'd looked into her eyes, Frisco held her other hand the entire trip—and prayed.

CHAPTER 4

Three hours later, Frisco, Hollywood, Reardon, Sawyer, his operative, Kip "Skipper" Morrison, and the chopper pilot, Tempest "Babs" Van Buren sat in Kearsarge's mess hall, waiting for news about Jane Jones—that was the only name for Haven that had been given to the staff who knew better than to dispute it. There would be no record of her ever having been aboard, and all the medical documents in her chart would leave with her. The crew was steadily bringing the ship closer to the Persian Gulf, northwest of the Arabian Sea. The less time Haven spent in the air following surgery, the better. Frisco just prayed she made it that far. She hadn't regained consciousness before being taken into surgery.

Glancing at Van Buren, a retired Air Force pilot

in her early or midthirties, Frisco had to agree with her handle, which was short for "bad-ass bitch." She'd flown like the hounds of Hell were nipping at their tail rotor, getting them to Kearsarge in record time, before battling some nasty crosswinds and high seas, left over from an earlier storm, during the landing. Even some of the ship's crew had remarked it was some of the best flying they'd ever seen under those conditions. The only person who hadn't agreed was Reardon who'd tossed his cookies a few times into a barf bag Sawyer had thrust into his hands.

It wasn't until after Haven was being whisked away on the gurney, which had been waiting for their arrival, that Frisco had gotten a good look at the other woman. As the brunette climbed out of the pilot's seat, he'd caught a glimpse of her titanium left leg. Later, Sawyer had told him how she'd lost it when an RPG had struck her helicopter in Afghanistan as she was extracting a bunch of Marines from a hot zone. Despite her leg being mangled, she'd managed to fly the damaged bird far enough away from the enemy before crash landing it. Every single one of the Marines had survived with, at worst, a few broken bones. By the time a second rescue crew had retrieved them, they'd had to apply a tourniquet to Babs's leg to keep her from bleeding to death. At the hospital, the limb had needed to be amputated just below the knee. After giving her time to recover and get her disability discharge, Sawyer had approached the woman, who'd flown him and others from SEAL Team Four on numerous missions. He'd offered her a job as both a helo pilot and fleet mechanic at Trident. Frisco had been impressed to learn the private company had its own Sikorsky MH-X Silent Hawk— an extremely expensive toy. Unfortunately, though, for this mission on the other side of the world, they'd had to borrow the Blackhawk from allies in the region. It must have cost a small fortune or a lot of payback markers to arrange it.

Taking another swig of the disgusting swill they called coffee around there, Frisco grimaced. Usually the Navy vessels had awesome coffee, but this tasted like it'd been brewed with a dirty sock for a filter. It was the middle of the night, and they'd been offered bunks to crash in, but everyone wanted to wait until the surgery was over. Aside from a few crew members coming in and out for various reasons, the six of them were alone. They'd been able to take showers and change into sweatpants and T-shirts purchased from the ship's store on Trident's tab.

Sawyer and Hollywood were both catching a combat nap in chairs to his left. Across the room, Reardon, Skipper, and Babs were monitoring the news the crew had patched into a closed-circuit-TV via the ship's satellite feed, even though the reception was sketchy at times.

The BBC was covering the story of the tragedy in India at what some people, newspapers, and magazines had been referring to, prior to today, as the Royal Wedding of the Year. So far, a reported twenty-seven people were dead, including the groom's father and brother, and scores were injured. Most of the deaths, some bodies burned beyond recognition, had occurred in the cigar bar, which'd been down the hall from the library where Haven and Reardon had been standing. The numbers were expected to rise as the authorities began to sift through the rubble of the mansion that had almost completely burned down after the two explosions had destroyed several rooms.

There was wide speculation about the tuxedoed men with guns found dead in the carnage of the building. Several hadn't been identified as being on the venue's security detail. There were also questions about the masked, militarized men, who'd emerged from the jungle, some of whom had been swooped up by a helicopter while kidnapping a couple. The others had disappeared back the way they'd come after the chopper had taken off. Some people were saying they'd been members of ISIS, others were blaming al Qaeda, and a few were saying it'd been British Special Forces getting revenge for recent attacks in London. It was almost surprising no one had suggested they'd been aliens from another planet. Frisco knew the Indian authorities would never be able to prove who'd actually been involved—Delta, Deimos, and Trident were that freaking good. Nothing had been left behind that could come back and bite them on the ass.

Frisco's mind kept flashing back to the moment when he'd realized Haven had been begging him to leave her to die. What had been going through her brain, at that very moment, to be filled with so much despair she'd given up hope in less time than most people decided what was for dinner, he didn't know. Leaving her hadn't been an option, whether she'd been dead already or just suffering from a hangnail. But the look of resignation in her eyes as she'd pleaded with him would haunt him to his dying day.

Multiple footsteps approaching had Frisco glancing toward the entrance to the mess hall. Ghost, Fletch, and a couple he didn't know walked in. The commanding officer of the ship had dispatched a chopper to retrieve them at Sawyer's request. Apparently, the retired SEAL had a lot of pull in the Navy—either that or he had friends in high places. Like the six that'd been onboard Kearsarge for several hours, the new arrivals had found somewhere to shower and change into comfortable civilian clothing. It was common to arrange for a safe house somewhere near the mission target in case things went to shit like they'd done earlier in the evening.

Hollywood instantly awoke and stood, scrubbing the sleep from his face, while Sawyer remained in his seat and held out a hand. "Ghost, I wish I could say it was nice to see you again."

The Delta Team leader snorted as he shook the other man's hand. "Same here, Sawyer. We sent your teams back with ours; they should be over the Atlantic by now. Your brothers said to say, and I quote, 'fuck you' for sending your jet to meet you in Bahrain. They're sitting in the back of a cargo plane and not too happy about it."

The other man scoffed. "Too fucking bad. Nick's name isn't on the letterhead, yet, and until it is, he's shit out of luck. And Dev's been getting too soft with his wife and kid. The trip will toughen him up again."

"Ian, how's Haven?" The exotic-looking woman's voice drew Frisco's attention. Her features had him thinking she was of South American descent, but he couldn't zero in on a specific country. With long, black hair pulled back into a ponytail, she stood about five foot eight on two-inch-heeled western boots. Her jean-clad legs seemed to go on for miles while her torso was covered by a long-sleeved, baby blue, V-neck T-shirt. She was physically fit, and Frisco had a feeling she wasn't a woman to be underestimated. Her companion, who had his arm possessively around her waist, was a tall, muscular but lean man, with dirty blond hair that fell unrestrained just below his shoulders. He was similarly dressed in jeans, a casual tee, and black biker boots and had that deadly aura about him those not in the special ops community might easily miss. This was a man not to be fucked with.

Sawyer shook his head. "Don't know. She's been unconscious since we loaded her onto the bird. She got hit in the middle of her back, really close to her spine. One of the nurses came out about twenty minutes ago and said they were wrapping things up. The surgeon's supposed to come out soon to talk to us. By the way, Taint-waffle, this is Jackass and Sweetheart. Hollywood has already had the pleasure."

Frisco rolled his eyes as he held out his hand. "Everyone else calls me Frisco."

The woman smiled as she shook his hand. "Everyone else calls me Jordyn, and this is Carter."

"Nice to meet you. Wish it was under better circumstances."

As Carter also gave him a handshake, Jordyn strode over to where the others were still watching the news. Reardon's attention had been so focused on the TV, he hadn't even noticed when she and the others had come in. When Jordyn put her hand on his arm, he startled, then stood and walked into her embrace. It was then the man finally broke down, having remained stoic all this time. His shoulders shook as he silently cried on her shoulder. From what Frisco had figured out earlier, Reardon was very protective of both female spies, like they were his older sisters or something. He'd spoken of both of them fondly over the past few hours to Babs, who'd tried to keep him engaged in conversation while they waited for news.

Giving the other two some privacy, Skipper and Babs walked over and joined the rest of them. After watching Jordyn and Reardon for a few moments, Sawyer stood and stretched. "Any news on the buyer?"

Carter crossed his arms over his sculpted chest. "No. We've narrowed him down to five possibles—one of whom is dead in the rubble. He was the one who shot Haven from the window of the library. Reverend took him out and, thankfully, didn't make it a head shot, so I was able to get a few photos from different angles before the authorities arrived and gained control of the place. We're running his face through the recognition program. No hits yet, but it could be hours before we get one."

Footsteps sounded again and, this time, a harried-looking man in scrubs strode in. He eyed the newcomers as Jordyn and Reardon hurried over.

"It's okay, Doc, they're family," Sawyer reassured him.

The older man nodded and took off his glasses. "I'm sure I don't want to know what kind of family it is. I have my orders that this case doesn't exist." He took in a deep breath and blew it back out. "She's being moved to recovery. The bullet nicked the spinal cord at L1 and 2, then lodged in the spleen, which we had to remove. The trauma around the spine has caused swelling and bruising. As a result, she's got cord shock. She can't feel anything below the injury right now, but I'm pretty sure it's temporary. Because of the muscles around the spleen, there may come a point where the pain and paresthesia will be more pronounced on her left side, but, again, that depends on her recovery."

"So she's going to be all right?" Reardon asked, hopefully.

The doctor shook his head. "I wish I could say that, but I can't. We won't know more until the cord heals to see if she'll regain full function. Will she be able to run again? I highly doubt it. Will she be able to walk with or without the assistance of crutches and braces? I think that's up to her and how her recovery goes. I've seen people regain full or limited use of their legs and lower abdominal organs, while others have given into depression or guilt or whatever's holding them back, and they're in a wheelchair for the rest of their lives. She's going to need a lot of rehab. It could be two months before she starts to regain feeling in her legs, it could be as long as two years. I wish I could give you more than that, but recovering from this type of injury is different for every patient."

The group was quiet for a moment while they

digested the diagnosis, as vague as it was, then Jordyn spoke up. "When can we see her, Doctor?"

"Give the nurses a few minutes to get her settled in recovery. I can let two people in to see her for only a moment. After that, you'll have to wait 'til morning." He glanced at the clock on the wall. "Actually, since it's 0200, late morning. We're going to keep her heavily sedated for the next eighteen to twenty-four hours, until she's stable enough to be medevaced to Bahrain and board a flight to Landstuhl. They'll ease her out of the drug-induced coma in Germany. That will ensure she doesn't move around at all."

Carter glanced at everyone else to see if they had any more questions, then turned back to the surgeon. "Thanks, Doc. Jordyn and I will be staying with Haven until she can be transported. The officer of the deck said he's got a couple of bunks for us; I'll make sure your staff knows where to find us."

"Good. Get some sleep. If anything changes, we'll let you know."

After the doctor left, a tense and remorse-filled silence filled the air, before Carter turned to Sawyer. "I spoke to McDaniel—he's in Washington, handling the backlash of this clusterfuck. As soon as Haven can handle the trip, we'll get her back to the States. Do me a favor and take Reardon with you. Someone from Deimos will meet you in Tampa and escort him back to California."

"No!"

Frisco wasn't the only one startled by Reardon's venomous shout. His face reddened as he continued. "I'm staying with Haven. She's my responsibility. She was protecting me, and it's because of me she's hurt. I'm not leaving."

Before Carter could answer, Jordyn stepped between the two men, facing the one who was near tears again, this time in anger as well as grief. She placed her hands on his shoulders and made sure she had his attention, before speaking in a calming tone as if she were dealing with a young child. "Kenny, no." He shook his head, but she persisted. "Listen to me. Listen. I promise you, we'll take good care of her, but we don't know who's looking for 'Preston Ward' right now. Your face ended up on several videos that were taken by cell phones. The ones we've seen on the internet are blurry, but we can't take the chance someone knows what you look like. Haven would tell you exactly what I'm telling you— you have to go back to the States in protective custody. Once you're at headquarters, and Haven's awake, I'll get the two of you on the phone so you can talk to her, but you can't stay with her—it's not safe. I swear, as soon as we can, we'll bring her home."

Reardon had tried to interrupt several times, but the woman hadn't let him get a word in. They all saw the moment he surrendered. His shoulders sagged as he, reluctantly, accepted the fact he had to leave. Frisco felt the same way even though he barely knew Haven, and she didn't even know his name. He wanted to stay with her until she woke up, to see with his own eyes she was okay, but it wasn't an option.

A few moments later, a surgical nurse came in. Carter gestured for Jordyn and Reardon to go see Haven. Once they were gone, Sawyer picked up the plastic bag his camos were in. Their weapons and equipment they'd had on them were still in the Blackhawk, which was sitting on one of the ship's helipads. Babs would fly Reardon and the Trident and Delta team members to Bahrain where Sawyer's luxury jet was apparently waiting for them. For once, Frisco, Ghost, Fletch, and Hollywood would be flying even better than first class.

"Let's get the hell out of here," Sawyer announced. "Carter, send the dweeb up to the chopper when he's done and call us if you need anything."

"Will do."

As the others said goodbye to the Deimos spy and then moved toward the door, Frisco held back a moment. Carter raised an eyebrow at him.

He cleared his throat. "Listen . . . um . . . I don't know if you can, and I understand if you can't, but I'd appreciate it if you . . . uh . . . if you could let me know how she's doing."

The other man cocked his head to the side and stared at him for a few seconds. Frisco refused to back down from the intense scrutiny. Finally, Carter nodded. "I'll do my best."

"Thanks." Without another word, he walked out the door. For some unknown reason, though, he felt like he was leaving a part of himself behind.

CHAPTER 5

AN INCESSANT BEEPING PENETRATED HAVEN'S MIND, annoying her as she floated amidst pure darkness. When she tried to push it away, it was replaced by something else . . . something that had her wanting to scream. Pain . . . white, hot, searing pain. She was either still alive or had been borne through the gates of Hell, and didn't know which was worse. *Where am I?*

Searching the darkness, she tried to find a clue to where she was and how to get out of there. But the agony was so excruciating, she couldn't move. Her legs wouldn't obey her mind and felt like they were submerged in a vat of lava. This was it. Her Hell. The one she deserved after all this time. Or was it?

There had to be a way out. A way to redeem herself. Before it was too late.

Her eyelids were being held down by five-pound weights, and it took all her energy to pry them open. Wherever she was, it was dark, but not as bad as the abyss she'd been in. She could move her arms, but her legs were restrained. Haven blinked, and her head and stomach swirled in nauseating circles, causing her to slam her eyes shut again.

I'm drunk. I have to be. All the signs are there. Nausea, dry mouth, pounding headache. But she never got drunk—at least, not since college. And why did the rest of her feel like it was on fire—her back and stomach were just as bad as her legs. Had she been in an accident? *Oh, God!* Was she in the hands of one of her enemies? Was she being tortured? If that was the case, she didn't want to wake up.

Wait. No. It hadn't been an accident. Screams. Gunshots. *Run, Kenny. Before it's too late. Hurry. Kenny, where are you? I'm his bodyguard. Where is he? If anything happened to that sweet kid, I'll never forgive myself.* Yes, he was a part of her world, but only on the periphery. He spent his time cocooned in the communications center at headquarters. His engagements with the enemies of the United States were done from behind a computer screen. He'd never killed someone in cold blood because the alternative was Americans dying at some bastard's hands. *Kenny. Damn it. Where are you?*

The beeping grew louder. Faster. She had to get out of here. Had to find Kenny.

Haven. Wake up, honey. You're going to be okay. I'm right here. Wake up. That's an order, Haven.

She knew that deep, rumbling voice. She knew him. He was a friend. She was safe with him. The knowledge calmed her, easing her panic. She forced her eyelids upward again and, this time, she managed to keep them open and not throw up. Her eyes focused and found the man sitting next to the bed she was laying on.

"Hey, it's about time you woke up."

Carter. His blue eyes were filled with a combination of concern and relief. Haven scanned the room. She was in a hospital, so she must have been right— she'd been in an accident. Opening her mouth, she tried to speak, but her tongue and lips were so dry, she began to cough, and that sent shards of pain shooting through her body again. That damn beeping of the monitor over her left shoulder increased too.

"Hey, easy, sweetheart. Here. Take a sip of water." He held a straw to her lips, and Haven closed them around it, drinking the cool liquid greedily. "That's it. Not too much."

Letting go of the straw, she swallowed several times. "Wh-What happened? Where am I?"

Before he had a chance to answer her, the private room's door quietly swung open, and Jordyn walked in on silent feet. Her face lit up when she noticed Haven. "Oh, thank God." Hurrying over, she handed her lover a brown, paper, deli bag as he stood and let her sit in the chair. "How do you feel?"

"Like I got hit by a Mac truck. I'm in pain from head to toe. What happened?"

For some reason, her words startled the other woman, which she knew from experience was hard to do. Before Haven could analyze Jordyn's surprised expression, it morphed into something akin to empathy. Placing the bag on a window shelf, Carter stepped over to the device attached to an IV pole next to the bed. He handed her a cable with a small box on the end. "Push the blue button if you're in pain."

Haven took it from him, but despite feeling like crap at the moment, she wanted a clear head while she found out what was going on. "What happened?" she repeated. "Where are we?"

"Landstuhl Medical Center. You've been out of it for two days." Reaching over the bed railing, Jordyn laid her hand on her arm. "What do you remember?"

Her brow furrowed as she tried to think past the pain. "We were . . . we were at the wedding. Kenny . . ." Her eyes went wide. "Oh, my God, is he okay? Where is he?"

"He's fine. He's already back in California."

A sigh of relief escaped her. "Okay. Good." She settled back down and concentrated. "Um . . . we were walking around." The memories started pouring in. "There was an explosion. Then men with guns came in. I shot one of them. Kenny and I jumped out the window, and we were running . . . I . . ." She shook her head slightly, but the nausea returning stopped her. "I don't remember anything after that. What happened?"

Jordyn bit her lip and then glanced at Carter. He leaned over and took Haven's hand. "You were shot in the back, sweetheart. Ian and a few others came running and got you and Reardon out of there on the Blackhawk. They flew you straight to Kearsarge where you had surgery, before being transported here." He paused, and Haven got a sick feeling in her stomach. "The bullet nicked your spinal cord, which caused swelling and bruising, but the doctors said the damage will heal in time."

Unable to fully comprehend what he was telling her, the only words that stood out were "spinal cord" and "damage." Her mouth dropped in horror. "Wh-What do you mean damage? What kind of damage?"

"Sh. Listen to me. Calm down. You're going to be all right." He squeezed her hand. "The doctors are calling it cord shock. It means that until the swelling goes down, and the tissue heals, you're going to have limited use of your legs for a while."

"Limited?" Her gaze went back and forth between the two of them as she tried to understand what he was saying. "You—You mean I'm . . . I'm paralyzed? But I can feel my legs . . . I can . . ." Staring at her covered legs, she tried to move them, but they just lay there. She shook her head so hard in disbelief it should have gone flying off her neck, and her nausea returned. "No . . . no . . . but I can feel them. They hurt. I . . . oh, God, they hurt! Why can't I move them?"

Panic was setting in again. Ignoring her friends, who were now both trying to calm her down with words that were no longer making sense to her, she ripped her hand from Jordyn's grasp and threw the covers off her legs. She gaped at them, willing them to move, but they didn't even twitch. A sob rose within her as tears rolled down her cheeks. *This can't be happening! They're wrong! Oh, God!*

CHAPTER 6

Two Months Later . . .

You wanted to see me, Captain?"

Ghost looked up from the pile of paperwork on his desk. "Yeah, Frisco. Come in and close the door. Have a seat."

Relaxing at the use of his nickname and not his rank, Frisco did as ordered and sat on one of the two gray, utility chairs across from the other man. He'd been a little surprised when his own captain had told him to report to Bryson's office. While they were in the same squadron and troop, Frisco was on a different team. However, they often trained together and went on the same missions depending on the number of Deltas needed. In fact, twenty minutes ago, he'd been in the base's gym where a bunch of guys from both teams had been working out. He'd just come out of the shower and thrown on a pair of tan BDUs—Battle Dress Uniform, the military's version of cargo pants—and a green "ARMY" T-shirt when his captain had told him to get his ass over here. Now, he waited patiently for the reason why.

Leaning back in his rolling desk chair, Ghost stared at him. "I got a call a little while ago that I thought you might be interested in."

"From whom?" He wracked his brains trying to think of anything he might be in trouble over, but he drew a blank. Plus the captain didn't appear pissed . . . more like bothered.

"A man with one name."

Carter. On the flight back to the States in the Trident Security jet, Frisco had learned a little bit more about T. Carter. Not much, but enough to know nobody knew what the T stood for, except maybe his woman, and he had a knack for being in the right place at the right time when people he cared about were in trouble. Frisco had also found out that as far as anyone not on the mission was concerned, the man didn't even exist. Being on Delta, Frisco knew all about not being able to tell anyone who he was and what he and his teammates did for their country. The only time he'd ever be able to tell anyone he was on Delta Force was if he had a wife, and even then, he wouldn't be able to tell her much past that—not that he was getting married anytime soon. Hell, he wasn't even dating anyone. And ever since that clusterfuck in India, he'd had a hard time thinking about any woman other than Haven. It'd been two months, and the only thing he'd been told was that after two weeks in the Landstuhl Medical Center, she'd been transported back somewhere in the US and was recovering. What that entailed, he had no idea.

Frisco sat up a little straighter. "About Haven?"

Picking up a Post-it note from his desk, Ghost reached across and handed it to him. "Apparently, Agent Caldwell is rehabbing not too far from us. She's over in Temple, at Everest Rehabilitation Hospital, and our friend thought you might want to visit her."

His heart thumped faster in his chest at the thought of seeing her again. He hadn't been able to get her out of his head and had even been dreaming of her at night. At first, they'd been nightmares—reliving the moment she'd been shot and then her begging him to leave her to die. The anguish in her brown eyes haunted him. Then at some point, his dreams had changed. They'd turned erotic. She'd no longer been lying in pain on that lawn, covered in blood, soot, and dirt. Instead, she'd been gloriously naked, inviting him into her bed. The first morning he'd woken up from one of those dreams with his hand around his stiff and throbbing cock, he'd been mortified. She'd been badly injured and paralyzed—which he hoped was temporary as the surgeon had suggested—and all his subconscious mind and body wanted to do was imagine her straddling his hips and riding him hard.

He was tempted to jump out of the chair and run to the door—the hospital was only about a half hour away—but he was under the impression the captain had more to say, so he forced himself to remain seated.

"This is off the record—not Captain to Sergeant. This is Ghost to Frisco, all right?" When Frisco nodded, he continued. "Are you okay with everything that happened that night? I know I asked you that on the plane and a few days after we got back, but . . . from what Hollywood told me, Haven wanted you to leave her there. That had to be tough."

It shouldn't be a surprise Ghost was asking him about it, but this was the first time Frisco was aware, despite everything happening at the time, that anyone else had overheard her pleas. He took a deep breath and let it out slowly. "Obviously, there was no way I was leaving her, but . . . Jesus, Ghost, the look in her eyes when she realized she couldn't move her legs—I don't think I'll ever forget it. I also can't help but think I made things worse with the roll, then running with her bouncing on my shoulder."

Leaning forward, the captain rested his arms on the desk in front of him. "Frisco, you didn't have a choice. If Hollywood had been the first one on his knees, and you were covering his six, he would've done the same thing. *I* would have done the same thing, and so would every other Delta out there. You can't live in the world of what-ifs when you didn't have a choice. You got her out of there alive, and she's got a fighting chance because of it." He paused. "To tell you the truth, I wasn't sure if I was going to pass that message onto you."

Frisco's eyes narrowed. "Why not?"

"Well, apparently, she's having a hard time dealing with everything. Instead of fighting to get back on her feet, Carter believes she's given up, like the doctor said some people do. But for some reason, he thinks a visit from you might help. Don't ask why, because I have no idea. I stopped trying to question his thought process a long time ago. But he knows her a lot better than we do. It's up to you if you want to go."

"I do." There had been no hesitation in his answer, even though he was as confused as Ghost about what Carter thought he'd accomplish by going to visit her. However, there was no way he was looking a gift horse in the mouth. He was finally going to see the woman he hadn't been able to stop thinking about. Maybe he should go and get some flowers for her . . . a get-well bouquet or something. Or maybe a teddy bear or balloons from the hospital gift shop. He mentally shook his head. No, those weren't anything a kick-ass woman like Haven would appreciate. He'd have to give it some thought on the way there. And he was definitely going straight there as soon as this conversation was over.

"All right," Ghost said with a nod. "I just hope it doesn't blow up in your face."

"What do you mean?"

"I mean, don't go there expecting too much. She may not want to see you."

Frisco hadn't thought about that. Hell, he wasn't even sure she'd remember him—she'd been conscious for no more than three or four minutes in his presence and filled with pain and fear. Well, he wouldn't know until he saw her, and now the urge to go running to the hospital was even stronger. He needed to see her. Was it because of his guilty feelings that maybe he'd caused more damage to her spine than the bullet? Or was it something more?

CHAPTER 7

THAT FUCKING HURTS, BITCH." HAVEN KNEW THE REAL
bitch was her, but she just wanted the physical therapist to stop manipulating her legs. There was no
point for them to put her through this day after day.
She'd never walk again. Hell, she couldn't even go to
the bathroom without assistance.

"Muscles have a way of being vindictive if you
don't keep using them," the thirty-something blonde
responded, just like she'd done twice a day for the
past six weeks. She brought Haven's left leg up and
bent it, then stretched the quadriceps, pushing her
knee toward her chest. "You may have given up on
your walking again, but I haven't. You've got to stop
putting yourself down. Your life is far from over, and
one of these days you'll realize you've got a lot to live

for. No one's going to think less of you because of your limitations, so there's no reason for you to. For as long as you're here, you're stuck with me doing these exercises to help keep your muscles healthy and strong, and get you moving again. If not, atrophy will set in."

Haven scowled at the woman. "Screw you. Don't tell me how I should feel. Until you're lying in a bed next to me, unable to stand or walk, then you have no fucking idea how I feel. I'd rather be dead than stuck here, helpless and in excruciating pain."

It'd taken a few days in Landstuhl for Haven to realize the doctors had been right—what she'd been feeling at first had been "phantom pain." From the waist down, it'd all been in her head. She'd watched them stick her feet and legs with sharp instruments, trying to elicit a response, and each time, she'd willed her lower limbs to respond, but it hadn't happened. People thought when a person became paralyzed they didn't feel anything, but many times, the brain filled in the blanks. It knew its body was injured and should be in pain, so it provided a fake substitute, which was just as bad, if not more so, as if it had been true.

Four weeks ago, she'd started getting sensation back, all the way to her feet, but it felt like a thousand ants were crawling up and down her legs, and she was hypersensitive to touch. It was even worse during these stupid therapy sessions. The doctors had told her it would begin to fade as the swelling and bruising around her spine continued to heal, but after four weeks, it hadn't happened, and she didn't think it ever would.

"Shall we try the gym tomorrow?" asked the therapist, Hannah Burke, as she returned Haven's legs to their original position, then pulled the blankets back over them.

"Nope." She'd flat out refused to go to the gym for therapy. She didn't want the pitying looks from other people when they saw her at her most vulnerable—in a wheelchair. Each morning, a nurse and orderly helped get her into the bathroom to use the freaking toilet. Then, as they stood outside the door, she had to do the Kegel exercises they'd taught her, while sitting on the toilet bowl, so she wouldn't shit and piss herself during the day. And it didn't always prevent that, so she was stuck wearing an adult diaper of all fucking things. Nope, there was no way she was leaving this room until McDaniel found her someplace to live with a fucking caretaker they could trust. Dealing with one person seeing her at her worst was preferable to a bunch of people.

Sighing loudly, Hannah stepped over to the box of antibacterial gel that hung on the wall and cleaned her hands. "You know, after a while, these four walls are going to come crashing down on you."

"I should be so lucky," she mumbled, turning the television back on loud enough to let the other woman know she was dismissed. As soon as Haven was alone again in her private room, she lowered the volume, then dragged the bedside table over her hips and thighs, and booted up her laptop. She trolled the news sites aimlessly, not sure what she was even looking for. She'd give anything to have a secure internet connection so she could look around in the Dark Web, but that hadn't been possible. Maybe when she got out of here. Something had been niggling her brain about what'd happened before the mission had gone to hell, but she couldn't figure out what it was. Most of what she remembered was coming to her in brief flashes with large gaps of nothingness.

Her hand froze over the keyboard. "*When* I get out of here," she said out loud to the empty room. "How the hell is that ever going to happen?"

Haven had no family left, like most of the operatives at Deimos, and outside the walls of headquarters, she didn't really have any friends. She'd never been in one place long enough to make any. And wasn't that just ducky—thirty-four years old, a fucking invalid, with no family or friends, and no longer employed. Well, that last part wasn't completely true. Her superior, Gene McDaniel, had assured her several times that she'd always have a job with the covert agency. They'd get her set up with a secure computer system, with all the bells and whistles, and she'd basically be an information specialist. While she wasn't on the same geek level as Kenny and the others back in California, she knew enough she'd been able to do her own research most of the time. If she hit a wall she couldn't climb, she'd called HQ. Haven still had contacts all over the world she could access, it just wouldn't be face-to-face anymore.

As much as she wanted to get the hell out of the hospital, she also feared it. Here, it was easy to rely on the staff to help her. But out there, she'd have to hire someone to cook her meals, help her get dressed and showered, get her on the damn toilet, and drive her around. And if that person failed to show up, then what would Haven do? At least, whoever it was had to be cleared by Deimos. She'd never been needy, far from it, but now she couldn't do most things she'd always taken for granted.

Her legs twitched as they now did several times a day, and her left knee hit the bottom of the tray, rattling it. The impact, while slight, still sent stinging pinpricks through her nerves, and she gritted her teeth until the pain eased again. She refused to take the narcotics or other analgesics anymore—they just made her sleepy and nauseous.

Surfing the net, she didn't look up when the door to her room swung open. The nurses, technicians, food servers, and janitors were in and out all day long and half the night. How the hell anyone was supposed to sleep in a freaking hospital wasn't a thought worth analyzing.

Whoever had come in cleared his throat. Haven ignored him while reading the latest news article, and the speculations within, about what had really happened at the "Royal Wedding of the Year." Same old bullshit. No one had a fucking clue, so they just made stuff up.

"Haven?"

His voice was deep and rumbling, and she was surprised and irritated when it sent a shiver down her spine. "Just leave whatever it is on the dresser."

"Excuse me?"

"Who the hell are you and what do you want?" She still hadn't looked up from the computer screen, but she could see the guy out of the corner of her eye. He was dressed in tan BDUs and a green T-shirt that had "ARMY" written across it. His hands were empty. With her experience, she knew the man could be deadly, if the situation called for it, but his body language said he wasn't a threat to her. She almost wished he was. Jordyn and Carter had refused to give her a loaded gun for protection— they were afraid she was going to eat a bullet. There was a twenty-four-hour, armed guard outside her door, instead. The only way this guy could have gotten in was if he was on the approved visitor list or verified he worked here with a scan of his thumb print. Either way, Haven wanted him gone.

He took a few steps closer. His stature and body language screamed military confidence, but the expression on his face was one of uncertainty. "You ... um ... you don't remember me, I guess. I'm Frisco ... I mean, my name is Lucas Ingram, but everyone calls me Frisco. It's the nickname my team gave me ... from the Army."

"Well, good for you. Now that that's settled, get out." She yanked out the elastic tie holding her hair in a ponytail, ran her fingers through the strands, and put it back up again.

Seconds ticked by, but he didn't move. Haven

used to have the patience of a saint—in her business, it was vital—but since she'd become incapacitated, she didn't have tolerance for anybody. Finally, she couldn't take it anymore and spared him a glance. "What do you want?"

He shrugged. "I'm sorry if I'm bothering you, but I just . . . I just wanted to see if you were okay."

Her eyes narrowed at him. He looked familiar, but she couldn't place him. Standing about six feet tall, he had a sculpted torso most men wished they had and most women wanted to touch. Through the thin, snug tee, she could see the hard curves of his pecs and shoulders. His arms were just as nice. Brown hair, that could use a trim, a beard and mustache that had to be a few days old, and wicked hazel eyes completed the tempting package. She'd always been drawn to the military type, even if they had the undercover look going for them. Bad boys didn't do it for her—she dealt with too many of them in her line of work . . . her old line of work. *Damn it.* "Why would you care?"

"Well, I was there that night . . . when you got shot. I've been wondering how you were doing."

As Haven glared at him, images raced through her mind too fast for her to grasp onto one for more than a second or two. *Pain. Screams. Total chaos. I can't* move. *Oh, God, I want to die. Those eyes. That voice.* Anger flowed through her veins. "You son of a bitch. You're the one who picked me up, aren't you? I told you to leave me! Look at me!" She shoved the table with her laptop on it to the side, sending it crashing into the wall, and pointed at her immobile legs. "I'm paralyzed, you piece of shit! You should have left me there! I should be dead! But no, you had to be a goddamn hero, didn't you? Well, fuck you, asshole! You want to know how I'm doing? I'm stuck in this bed for the rest of my miserable life, that's how I'm fucking doing! Now, get the hell out of here!"

She was shouting so loudly her throat hurt, but didn't care. The guards had apparently gotten used to her temper tantrums because they no longer came running when they heard her yelling. As long as "help" wasn't part of her rant, they wisely stayed outside.

As Frisco stared at her, the blood drained from his face, and guilt filled his eyes. *Well, good, he should feel guilty. If it wasn't for him, I wouldn't be facing the rest of my life in a wheelchair. I'd be six feet under, which was a lot more preferable than this fate.*

His gaze dropped to the floor as his shoulders slumped. He took several deep breaths, before reaching behind his back. Haven knew it was useless to hope he was drawing a gun to shoot her, but, damn, she wished he would. Instead, he pulled something else from his waistband, took a few steps closer to her, and laid it on the bed next to her right thigh. She didn't look at it. Her fists and jaw clenched as she glowered at him.

He bit his bottom lip and lifted his gaze to hers again. And, God help her, all she saw was sorrow as he said, "I'm sorry you hate me, but if I had to do it over, I still wouldn't have left you there. I hope someday you can forgive me. Goodbye, Haven."

The man turned on his heel and strode across the room. Without a backward glance, he yanked open the door and walked out, letting it close again.

Moments passed before Haven's gaze slowly fell to the object he'd left. It was a rolled-up, black T-shirt. Her hands shook as she reached for it. Holding it by the shoulders, she let it unravel. She swallowed hard, and her stomach sank as she read the white lettering that said, "WAKE UP, KICK ASS, REPEAT."

CHAPTER 8

MYRIAD EMOTIONS COURSED THROUGH FRISCO AS HE strode out of the room and right smack into two people who'd been standing outside the door with the guard who'd let him in earlier. It was evident from their frowns that Carter and Jordyn had over-heard Haven yelling at him—hell, the whole floor must have heard her. His eyes narrowed. "You knew she was going to throw me out, didn't you?"

Carter sighed. "I had a feeling she would, yeah."

"So why the fuck did you call and ask for me to come?"

Before the other man could answer, Jordyn held up her hand. "This isn't the place for this discussion. Babe, why don't you take Frisco across the street for lunch? Meanwhile, my bitch of a friend is about to have a 'come to Jesus moment,' right before I kick her ass. Enough is enough."

Her jaw was clenched as she gave Frisco a pat on his shoulder, then pushed her way into the room.

"Come on." Carter gestured toward the elevators. "I'm buying."

He snorted as they started down the hall. "It's the least you could freaking do."

Five minutes later, they were sitting in a booth at the bar of a TGI Fridays. A pretty, blonde waitress smiled at the two men as she took their order. A few months ago Frisco would have been all over her, flirting and asking her out, but since India, there was only one woman he wanted to see, and she'd just thrown him out of her hospital room.

Once they were alone, Carter leaned forward and crossed his arms on the table. "I'm sorry about that, but I was afraid if I warned you, you wouldn't have come."

The man took a deep breath and let it out. "Do you know what Dominants and submissives are?"

His eyes narrowing, Frisco replied, "Like in BDSM? Yeah, I've heard of it. A few Deltas are into it, and I know Ian Sawyer and his brother own a club down in Tampa. He told me if I was ever in the area to stop by and see the place, but it's not my thing. What's it got to do with Haven and why I'm here?"

"It's not for everybody, but it'll hopefully help me get my point across. There are different levels in the lifestyle, and each couple negotiates the terms of their relationship. But no matter what, it's a Dom's job to make sure their sub gets what he or she needs, and that may not always be in sync with what they want. There's a high level of trust needed between the two of them. You're interested in her, that's plain to see, and I've gotten the impression it's more than a passing fantasy. While neither one of you is in the lifestyle, you could use the theory behind it to help her get past this funk she's in. She needs to let go of her anger and fear, stop overthinking everything, and realize she's still a desirable woman who can still do things most people can. She needs a reason to take a step forward in the right direction."

Carter paused as the waitress came back with their frosty mugs of tap beer. He winked at her. "Thanks, darlin'." As she walked away with a blush across her cheeks, he shook his head in disbelief. "Jeez, I've been in Texas, on and off, for six weeks, and I'm talking like freaking Egghead. Shoot me now."

"It's infectious. When I go home to San Francisco, my buddies all make fun of my twang."

Carter smirked before continuing. "All right, back to Haven. I assume you know the seven stages of grief." Swallowing a mouthful of beer, Frisco nodded. "Shock or disbelief, denial, anger, bargaining, guilt, depression, and finally acceptance and hope. Well, Haven is stuck on those first three stages. I was hoping if she saw you as a human being and not just someone to blame for what wasn't your fault, she'd start getting past it. She really is a sweetheart, but this has her spiraling out of control, and I'm afraid she's going to find a way to end it all." He shrugged. "I'm not sure I'd react any differently in the same situation—being an operative is all I know. And in our agency, there are very few friends and even fewer family members, if any, to rely on in situations like this. But Haven's refusing to even try to get on her feet again. It's like she feels this is her penance for something. What, I don't know. Like most of the agents at Deimos, including myself, her past can't be connected to her present. As far as anyone who knew her before she came to us knows, she's dead. She was given a new name and background history. The only two people, that I'm aware of who know of her life back then are McDaniel and the agent who trained her. Unfortunately, Luis Benito is dead.

Having been a part of the black-ops community for the past few years, Frisco wasn't surprised Haven wasn't her birth name, but it did make him even more curious about her. Not that it did him any good now.

"Anyway," Carter continued, "the only person Haven hasn't gone off on over the past two months is Reardon—he calls her a few times a week. From what I hear, he's dealing with his own misplaced guilt about what happened that night. He's the only one Haven puts on a front for—pretending everything is hunky-dory when it's not. Everyone else is subjected to her wrath. My boss has already located a house for her nearby that's wheelchair accessible, but until she's able to take care of herself with little assistance, she's going to be bedridden. Jordy and I have been doing everything we can, but she's fighting everyone. I don't know what else to do."

As the man stopped to take a drink of his beer, Frisco pondered everything he'd said. "Well, I doubt my visit made a difference. You obviously heard her throw me out."

"Maybe. But maybe it *did* make a difference. It may not have been what she wanted, but, instead, what she needed—and it might take a bit for that to sink into her thick skull. Just don't hate her for what happened back there, because if she does finally reach that last stage of acceptance, she might want to make amends. And I think that's something you'll need, too."

Frisco doubted that would ever happen, but a kernel of hope was planted in his heart. He just wished it would see the light of day sometime in the future.

"I cannot believe you. Are you out of your goddamned mind? Wait, don't answer that, because it's obvious to everyone around you that you are."

Dropping the shirt into her lap, Haven rolled her eyes. "Go away, Jordyn. I'm not in the mood for you right now."

"Well, too fucking bad." She tossed her small purse on an empty visitor's chair. "Unless you can get out of bed and kick me out of this room, you're stuck with me, because I sure as hell am not going to leave like that poor guy just did until I've said my piece."

Haven's eyes blazed with rage. "That's a shitty

thing to say to someone who's paralyzed! Don't you think I want to get out of this bed?"

"No, I don't." Jordyn took two steps forward, crossed her arms over her chest, and cocked her hip to the side. "If you really wanted to get out of that bed, you'd be down in the physical-therapy gym every chance you got, doing *everything* you could to get back on your feet again. All I see here . . ." She gestured to Haven's broken body lying on the mattress. ". . . is someone who's given up, wallowing in self-pity. I see someone who *I know* can kick ass suddenly rolling over and playing dead. It's fucking pathetic, Haven, and as of today, I'm not going to stand by and watch you spiral down into a pit of destruction. Until you get off your butt, literally, and start taking your life back, I'm done, and so is Carter. We want to be here for you, but I refuse to be treated like a piece of shit, nor am I going to watch you treat anyone else that way. That man . . ." She pointed to the door. ". . . that heroic, yet incredibly sweet man was the first one running across that lawn to get to you. He even beat Ian, who was hauling his own ass to cover your six and get you and Kenny out of there. You begged Frisco to leave you and let you die. How fucking dare you do that to someone like him . . . or anyone else, for that matter? Frisco's not some wet-behind-the-ears kid trying to play Superman. He's lost teammates on the battlefield—had them shot and killed two feet away from him—watched them get blown up in the Humvee directly in front of the one he was in." It wasn't surprising Jordyn knew his background. If he'd been allowed into Haven's room, someone had to have cleared him.

"No one survived in the vehicle he was *supposed* to be in. Because of a damn joke, he ended up in the other one. He grieved, and then he got his ass back in the game so their lives were not taken away in vain. He'd give anything to have his buddies back again, and you . . . *you* turn around and beg him to leave you to the same fate they didn't have a choice about! How fucking dare you put him in that position? He risked his life for you and Kenny, and then he held your hand the entire chopper ride to the ship and wouldn't let go until he had to when you were passed off to the surgical staff. And he's been worried about you ever since, according to his teammates. He didn't shoot you, and I'll be damned if I allow you to blame him for anything."

Jordyn shook her head as if she'd come to a sad conclusion. "You know what? You're not the person I thought you were. I remember watching Luis Benito train you. No matter what he threw at you, you worked your ass off until you had it down pat—hand-to-hand, shooting, the obstacle course, everything. Luis must be rolling over in his grave right now, disappointed about how his favorite protégé just gave up when the going got tough. If you want to continue having a pity party for the rest of your life, don't invite me, because I'm fucking done. Call me if you decide to return to the land of the living."

Without giving Haven a chance to say another word, Jordyn grabbed her purse, spun on her heel, and stormed out of the room. The sudden silence that filled the air, as the door slowly closed behind her friend, grew more oppressive as seconds and then minutes passed. For the first time in Haven's life, she felt truly alone, and that was saying a lot considering she had no family left and few friends. Her gaze fell on the T-shirt still in her lap. *Wake up, kick ass, repeat.* She took a deep, shuddering breath and let it out while staring out the window.

She wasn't sure how much time had gone by before the door swung open again and her lunch was brought in. The young woman, whose name tag read Shanell, eyed her warily, and Haven realized she was waiting to be bitched at for something. *God, you've been a real ass to everyone.*

The hospital employee carefully put the tray

down on the second bedside table Haven had insisted on, since her laptop was always on the other one, and wheeled it over to the bed. Before she could move away, Haven reached out and grabbed her hand. Startled, the woman's eyes went wide. Haven tried her best to put a warm smile on her face. "Thank you for bringing my lunch. I'm sorry I've been a bitch to you and everyone else. It's not fair to any of you."

Shanell's shoulders relaxed, and she squeezed Haven's hand. "It's okay. You've been through a lot. I hope this means you're ready to get better."

"I hope so too."

CHAPTER 9

Six months later . . .

Groaning, Frisco climbed out of his truck. His shoulder was stiffer than usual this morning, and he couldn't wait until the physical therapist put the damp, heated pad on it to loosen it up. Three weeks after badly straining the trapezius muscle that ran down his neck to his left scapula, during a rescue operation in Syria, he'd finally regained full range of motion of his arm again. But last night, he must have slept wrong because when he'd woken this morning, it felt like he'd pinched a nerve or something. Hopefully, it wasn't going to delay his recovery—he didn't want to miss out if his team got called up for another mission. So far, he'd been lucky.

Striding across the parking lot of the Carl R.

Darnall Army Medical Center in Fort Hood, he reveled in the cooler air that a weather front had ushered in last night. It was the first time in weeks the temperature had dropped below ninety degrees. When he entered the lobby, the air conditioning caused goosebumps to pebble across his skin, and a shiver went down his spine. Knowing the way to the physical therapy department by heart, he headed down the correct hallway and made two rights and then a left.

The older civilian receptionist greeted him with a smile as he entered the waiting area. "Hi, Frisco. You can go on back. You're on cot number two."

"Thanks, Mrs. Schaffer."

As usual, the huge PT room was filled with a number of physical therapists and their aides working on men and women who were recovering from various injuries, some worse than others. Several patients were on the treadmills and stationary bikes, while others were doing stretches and exercises on other equipment. One man, with a prosthetic leg, was using the parallel bars for support as he took steps toward a waiting wheel-chair he was probably working to get out of permanently.

Ordinarily, Frisco came in the mornings, but

due to a scheduled 0900 team meeting, he'd asked for an afternoon appointment. Climbing up on his assigned cot, he waited for someone to bring a TENS unit—an electronic nerve stimulator—and a heating pad for him. Tilting his head from side to side, Frisco winced in annoyance as a sharp pain shot through the left side of his neck. "Damn it," he muttered. But there was no way he was complaining about it louder than that, not with all of those recovering from far worse injuries than his nearby.

He glanced around the room, and a brown-haired woman in a wheelchair, with her back to him, caught his eye. She'd turned her head just enough for him to see a partial profile, and there was something familiar about her that caused him to stare, waiting for a chance to see her face to identify her. As if sensing a gaze upon her, she grabbed the wheels and spun the chair around, just as his regular therapist, Chad Walker, called out from across the room, "Hey, Frisco. I'll be right there."

Giving the man a distracted wave, Frisco's heart pounded in his chest when a set of soft, brown eyes met his hazel ones. A flash of uncertainty was replaced by recognition on the pretty woman's face, and he was shocked when the corners of her mouth ticked upward before she pushed on the chair's wheels, propelling herself toward him.

Haven. The woman he still hadn't been able to get out of his mind all these months. He'd even tried to hook up with a chick he'd met in a bar one night a few weeks ago, but it hadn't felt right, even though she'd appeared to be a sure thing. Instead of taking her up on the offer to go back to her place, Frisco had politely declined, to her obvious disappointment. Now, he was glad he had.

Haven stopped at the end of the cot he sat on and cocked her head. "Frisco Ingram?" When he silently nodded, still trying to convince himself she wasn't an apparition, she continued. "You didn't have that full beard the last time I saw you. It was much shorter then."

A grin spread across his face, gaining one from her too, as he realized she was wearing the T-shirt he'd given her all those months ago. It was a little big on her, but she didn't seem to mind. He ran a hand down his whiskers. "Yeah, it definitely needs a trim. How are you, Haven? You're here for therapy, I assume." He was a little surprised since it was a military facility, but there were too many people around to ask her about that. No one there knew he was Delta, and he had to assume no one knew she was from Deimos, an agency most, if not all, of those in the room had never heard of.

"Yeah, I am. Finally got off my sorry ass and decided to come back to the land of the living, as my friend Jordyn says." She paused, her mouth flattening again as contrition filled her eyes. "Um . . . look, I'm sorry about what I put you through—both the night I was shot and then again at the hospital. You didn't deserve any of that. I was the ultimate bitch to you. This . . ." She gestured to her legs. ". . . isn't your fault. The damage was done by a bastard who's hopefully rotting in Hell. I shouldn't have taken my fear and anger out on you. I really am sorry. Thanks for getting me and Kenny out of there alive."

Frisco sat up straighter, feeling lighter than he had in the past eight months. "Apology accepted. I'm glad to see you're doing okay and not carrying around a death wish anymore. How's everything going?"

"You mean my legs?" He nodded again. "Actually, better than I expected. The swelling has gone down around my spine, and they're working on getting me up on my feet again with braces and crutches. The doctors and therapists think I'll be able to kick this chair to the curb one of these days.

It's hard work, but not much harder than my training."

He didn't doubt that. From what he'd learned from Carter, Jordyn, and Sawyer, Haven had been a hell of an operative, able to take down men twice her size, who'd been dumb enough to underestimate her. He suspected she could still take someone down, despite her injury, given enough motivation. And, damn, that thought turned him on. Even with her long hair pulled up into a ponytail and without a stitch of makeup on, she was prettier than he remembered, which was saying a lot. He was still having erotic dreams about her a few times a week. He couldn't help it—his subconscious seemed to be in that movie *Groundhog Day*, where it just kept repeating itself. His cock twitched in his BDUs as he recalled what his fantasy Haven had been doing to him just that morning, and he mentally ordered it to behave.

"So, what are you doing here?" she asked. "Where's your boo-boo?"

His grin spread wide as he chuckled. "My boo-boo? I haven't had one of those since I was five or six and my mom kissed my skinned knee to make it better. But the reason I'm here is a strained muscle that's, literally, a pain in the neck."

"Hmm. At least it's not a pain in the ass." She snickered. "Sorry, bad pun."

A bark of laughter escaped him. He was thrilled she felt comfortable enough to crack a joke with him. "Yeah, that was pretty bad. But, tell you what— you can make it up to me by letting me take you to lunch." *Please don't shoot me down.*

Her eyebrows flew upward as she was clearly surprised by his invitation. "What? When?"

"Are you still in the middle of your treatment or can you stick around for a bit? We can go after Chad is done torturing me." Having overheard the sarcastic remark, the therapist smirked as he approached with a TENS unit and a heating pad.

"Torture? Nah, Chad doesn't torture anybody," Haven said. "Just be grateful Clarissa, aka Attila the Hun, over there, isn't your therapist—I think she's a sadist or something. All she's missing is a leather whip and over-the-knee boots."

Glancing to where she pointed, Frisco had to agree the six-foot-tall, female therapist did look like she knew a thing or two about intel retrieval via pain. His gaze returned to Haven, where it heated. "So, lunch?"

Once again, she caught him off guard as a pink blush appeared on her cheeks, but she still kept eye contact with him. "Um . . . sure. Actually, you might be able to help me with something."

"What?"

She gave a quick glance over her shoulder when her name was called. "We'll talk about it later. Attila is calling me. It's time for me to learn how to tap dance again—not that I ever knew how to do it before."

For the next hour, while he did his own exercises and received treatment, Frisco watched in awe as braces were attached to Haven's legs, and, with help from the therapist and one of the aides, she stood and used all her strength to support most of her weight with her upper body while "walking" from one end of the parallel bars to the other. Her lean arm muscles bulged as she struggled to place one hand and then the other further down the bars, before taking one step and following it with a second. She then started the whole one-two-three-four process over and over again. Sweat covered her face, but it was out-shined by her determination.

By the time Frisco's appointment was over, Haven was lying on her back as Clarissa massaged her thin legs. It would take more therapy before the muscle tone was built up again, but she was definitely on her way to a decent recovery. He was glad to hear the doctors still believed she'd walk again. She'd been lucky—a millimeter in the wrong direction and that wouldn't have been a possibility. As she laughed and joked with the others in the room, Haven seemed okay with the fact she wouldn't get one-hundred percent use of her legs back and was willing to take as much as she could get. Damn, he was proud of her—she'd gone from wanting to be dead to looking like she was ready to take on the world again.

When she sat up at the end of her treatment, he handed her a clean towel he'd grabbed from a nearby shelf. She thanked him, then wiped her face with it. "Do you mind if we get takeout for lunch? After sweating my ass off, I really don't want to sit in a restaurant. Or maybe we better do this some other time," she added as she deftly swung herself into the wheelchair the PT aide had moved closer to the cot.

"No worries. Takeout is fine with me." Frisco wasn't going to let this opportunity slip through his fingers. He'd been dreaming of her for months and now he was afraid if he let her go, he'd never see her again.

"Okay." Haven wheeled her chair around him and headed for the door. "See if you can keep up, slacker."

Frisco grinned as he hurried to catch up to her. "Slacker, huh?"

They continued out to the parking lot, chatting about everyday things, just like any ordinary couple, which they were so far from being. Haven and Frisco had seen and done too many things for their country to be considered "ordinary." Maybe that was another reason Frisco felt such a strong attraction to the female operative—she understood what it was like to be someone who had to keep his true professional life a secret from the public world. While there were many missions neither could give details about, they'd be able to talk in general terms and have the other fathom what they'd gone through.

Haven stopped next to a van parked in a handicap spot near the front entrance to the hospital. "It's probably easiest if you follow me. I know a little shack with great burgers right next to a park we can eat in."

"You're driving?" When her eyebrows shot up, he scrambled to cover his faux pas. "I mean, it's great that you are. There's no reason you shouldn't . . . I mean, I'm just surprised you can . . . um . . . that came out wrong . . . sorry, but how . . ."

She held up a hand to stop him from babbling further. "How do I use the pedals when I don't have full control over my legs, yet? The driver's setup has been modified with an accelerator and brakes I control with my hands. It took a shit ton of lessons to get used to it, but, so far, I haven't run over any little old ladies—so all's good.

"That's always a good thing." He was relieved she hadn't taken offense to his shock and questions. Pulling his keys out of his pocket, he said, "All right, then. I'm parked a few rows over in a navy-blue Charger. I'll meet you at the exit."

"Muscle car, huh? And here I thought you were a pickup man."

CHAPTER 10

PUTTING THE VAN IN PARK IN A HANDICAPPED SPACE that gave her the room she needed, Haven took a moment to collect herself. The last person she'd expected to walk into the PT gym today was Lucas "Frisco" Ingram. Not wanting Carter and Jordyn to know she hadn't been able to stop thinking about the guy since he'd come to visit her in the hospital, she'd asked Kenny to get her the intel on him. A few weeks later, when she'd been released and moved into the handicapped-accessible home the US government had acquired for her, complete with secure internet access, she'd done her own research on him . . . not that she found much more than Kenny had given her. Her favorite thing to look at was Frisco's high school yearbook she'd found online. He was a hunk back then, too, and had been voted "Nicest Eyes" and "Homecoming King." He'd been one of three co-captains on the varsity football team and, when they'd won the state championship, been named MVP after breaking the school record for rushing yards by a running back. Haven was sure she would've been even more impressed if she knew what a running back was and why he was rushing. Football wasn't her thing.

Unlocking her chair from behind the steering wheel, she rolled back to the side door and slid it open. Frisco had parked in a regular spot nearby. He now stood and watched as she secured the chair to a platform that would move her out of the vehicle and lower her to the ground. It was a slow process, but one she'd gotten used to. Hopefully with a few more months of healing and therapy, she'd be able to ditch the specially-equipped van altogether.

After the lift went back into the van, Haven shut the door, then wheeled over to Slim's Shake Shack —a hamburger, hot dog, and malted shake stand that operated from the back of a large, converted, box truck—in the corner of the parking lot. The owner was a retired fireman who made some of the best damn burgers she'd ever had. She'd found the little hut one day when Jordyn had been in town without Carter, who'd been on a mission. The two women had taken advantage of the comfortable weather and decided to go for a stroll—or roll in Haven's case—around the lake that was at the center of the park.

After placing their orders, Frisco refused to take money from her, treating her to lunch. Once they had their burgers and sides, they doctored them up with condiments set on a shelf next to the cut-out window of the truck. Haven then put their cans of soda on her lap and followed Frisco, who carried their plates, over to a picnic table in the shade of a tall elm tree. Wanting to be on the same level as him, Haven locked the wheelchair, set the sodas on the table, then easily transferred herself onto the wooden bench across from her lunch date.

It was a beautiful day, something Haven never thought she'd enjoy again. While the sun was shining high in the sky, the temperature was only in the low 80s.

"If these things taste as good as they smell, I'll be in heaven," Frisco said as he placed her plate in front of her.

"I guarantee you'll love it. I come here at least twice a week to get one."

"Well, that explains why Slim knew your name

and didn't need to ask what you wanted beyond 'the usual.'"

She dipped a french fry into a blob of ketchup and smirked at his comment. "Yeah, go figure. For years I made sure nothing I did was out of habit. No patterns for anyone to follow and use to ambush me. Now, I'm doing a lot of the same stuff each week. Although, I do take a different route each time I go anywhere. Some habits die hard."

Frisco took a huge bite out of his "Double Down" burger—two beef patties, pepper jack cheese, bacon, and fried onions topped with barbecue sauce—and moaned loudly through his full mouth. Haven chuckled, knowing exactly how he felt.

"Told ya," she said before digging into her own avocado-topped burger. They ate in a comfortable silence for several minutes while Haven studied the man who'd saved her life, despite her protests at the time. His medium-brown hair was even longer than she remembered, as was his beard, but she'd recognize those wicked, hazel eyes anywhere, especially when they were focused on nothing but her.

"So . . ." he started between swallowing a mouthful and taking a sip of his cola. "What did you need my help with?"

Haven took a deep breath and let it out slowly.

What she was about to ask him was going to bring back a lot of bad memories for both of them. "I need you to tell me what happened that night, from your point of view."

His hand had been halfway to his mouth with three french fries when it froze. He frowned as he stared at her. "What? Why?"

"I'm hoping you can jog my memory. Nothing else has worked." She glanced around to make sure they were completely alone . . . one of those habits that wouldn't die. "Apparently I recognized someone who shouldn't have been there right before the explosion. Kenny said it was one of two guys we saw in the hallway before we entered the library. I was waiting for them to either follow us in or walk past the door so I could get a better look. But neither of those things happened before the explosion went off. I've looked at the surveillance videos we recovered but nobody stuck out who hasn't been identified already. I'm sure you heard that some of the video feeds had been tampered with, and half the footage is nothing but static or blank."

"Yeah, Ghost—Captain Bryson, who was on lead for my team for the mission—mentioned it a few months ago. Said they still haven't figured out who has the nuke. Whoever it is has gone silent, not even popping up on the Dark Web."

"It's driving the Deimos intel techs nuts. They've been searching for any sign of the nuke or Mr. Smith with no results. I've gone through all the available videos and still photos. I've spoken to every Deimos and Trident Security operative that was there. Hell, I even had the agency shrink hypnotize me. Nothing. It wasn't the bastard that shot me, nor was it the guy I killed before we jumped out the window. We've identified both of them and gone through their known associates. Still, zilch. So, since you're one of the few people I haven't spoken to yet about that day, I was hoping something or someone you saw will help jog my memory. I remember leaving the ballroom, but after that, everything is just flashes of moments, nothing consistent." However, those gorgeous eyes of his were one thing she hadn't forgotten.

"I don't know how much I can help since I was in the jungle for most of it, but if you think it might work, okay." He popped the last bite of his burger into his mouth, then pushed the plate of fries to his right. Resting his elbows on the table, he swallowed, then took a deep breath. "God, this is weird. It's rare I can talk about a mission outside the Deltas—hell, I can't even tell most people I *am* Delta—but I was told that you, and the rest of your agents, are cleared for intel sharing about that mission."

She completely understood that. There were very few people in the world, who didn't work for Deimos, she could discuss her assignments with.

"All right, let's see. We didn't know you all were there until Sawyer joined Hollywood and me and we merged the two communication systems." Frisco proceeded to give her a rundown of what he remembered from that point, most of which she'd heard already from her fellow agents and the Trident teams. He paused a moment to take another sip of his soda. "We'd just gotten a photo of you and Reardon—by the way, you rocked that dress."

Another blush spread across her face. *What the hell?* She never blushed, and here she was doing it repeatedly in this man's presence. She was attracted to him, that she couldn't deny. However, she couldn't help but think it was a warped case of hero worship, even though she hadn't wanted him to save her life when they'd first met. And she was sure the attraction was one-sided. He obviously liked to flirt, but her wheelchair had to be a complete turn-off, didn't it?

Frisco continued as if he hadn't just given her the

compliment. "I remember you starting to say something moments before the explosion, but we couldn't make out what. You'd said a word or two, so we knew it was you talking, then there was a burst of static. Sawyer asked you to repeat it, but from the sound of things you couldn't."

Haven nodded her head. "Kenny said two couples had gotten drinks at the bar in the library, then stepped closer to us so I couldn't repeat whatever I'd said, which apparently was that I wanted to get a better look at the guy I recognized."

"But you never saw him again."

"No. What happened after the explosion?"

"Total chaos. People screaming and running outside. I never saw you jump out of the window, there were too many people coming out on our side. Every operative was looking for you. Sawyer's teams were about to break cover and go help evacuate while looking for you, when suddenly your dress caught my eye. You and Reardon were running straight for us. You'd either kicked off your shoes or lost them. You were limping but still moving quickly, covered in soot and blood." He pointed to her left forearm, which bore a faint scar. "Your arm was bleeding. I—I barely heard the shot, but I saw the . . . the moment you were struck."

His last few words came out as a hoarse whisper, and he swallowed hard. Haven had to hold back her tears at the sight of this strong man having a moment of grief over the recollection of the event that changed her life completely. She reached across the table and took his hand in hers. They sat in silence as they both struggled to regain their composure. Finally, Frisco cleared his throat. "Sorry about that. After all my missions and being on the front lines of battlefields, you'd think I'd be used to it, but it never gets any easier when you see that, even if it's a teammate you barely know or, in our case, hadn't met yet."

"Jordyn told me you've lost teammates before."

Sadness filled his eyes as the memory of those men clearly swirled to the forefront of his mind. He squeezed her hand. "Yeah. Seven of them in two separate incidents, although even one is too many."

Laughter broke the tension hanging in the air as two young children ran past their table toward the lake, while their mother shouted for them not to get wet from where she was spreading out a blanket on the grass nearby.

Frisco cleared his throat again. "Anyway, back to that day. I saw you falling, knew what'd happened, jumped to my feet, and ran toward you."

Before he could say anything more, she interrupted him. "You can skip the part where I was an ungrateful bitch."

The corners of his mouth turned upward. "Okay, skipping that part. After that, Hollywood and Sawyer covered us. Sawyer's sniper, Donovan, took out the shooter, and then the Trident helicopter swooped in to extract us. And if you haven't met Babs yet, I'll tell you, that woman is freaking awesome. Definitely earned her handle for being a bad-ass bitch. She landed the Blackhawk and got us out of there in record time."

"I haven't had the pleasure, yet, but I've heard all about her. So, that's it? Nothing else stands out?"

"No," he answered while shaking his head. "Sorry. But you know that when the shit hits the fan it's hard to recall specifics afterward. I can review my report and see if I forgot anything."

Haven shook her head. "Don't bother; I've already read it and everyone else's from that day."

Frisco snorted. "I can't imagine what security clearance you have for that—and I'm probably better off not knowing. So, I guess my stroll down memory lane didn't help, did it?"

"Unfortunately, no. Who knows, maybe I didn't know the guy and just thought he looked familiar."

"But you don't think that's the case, do you?"

"No." Haven suddenly realized Frisco was still holding her hand as if he'd been doing it for years. She wasn't sure if he knew his thumb was caressing her wrist. The gentle rhythm was sending sparks to the nerve endings under her skin, through her body, straight to her core. While she didn't have full use of her legs yet, the feeling had returned to her lower abdomen and all the way to her toes—and everything in between. And right now, what she felt between her legs was lust and desire. Before the shooting, she would've acted on that, seducing him until she got what she wanted—him in her bed. She'd always been picky about which men she hooked up with, even dating a few for several months or enjoying an occasional friends-with-benefits relationship. But since the wheelchair next to her had become such a huge part of her life, she hadn't been attracted to any male—until now. Why this man? He'd seen her at her absolute worst. She'd begged him to do what he considered to be an unspeakable act, yet, here he was, having granted his forgiveness, enjoying lunch with her.

Pulling her hand from his, and immediately missing the warmth of the contact, Haven stacked their plates together. "I really need to get back to work. I'm an intel tech now." While she wasn't as adept as some of the hackers and specialists at Deimos headquarters, she was still able to gather a lot of information needed by the field operatives. Her field experience helped because she was able to zero in on intel they needed instead of making them weed through the excess it was buried under. "Thanks for lunch."

"My pleasure." Grabbing the plates and empty soda cans, Frisco stood and tossed them into a nearby trash can before returning to the table, while Haven got situated back into her chair. "So, why here?"

His question threw her off as she began to propel the wheelchair toward her van. "Huh? Why here, what?"

"From what I understand, your headquarters is somewhere in California, so why are you in Texas?"

"Ah. Even though the main compound is out west, we have operatives all over the States, preferably near military bases in case backup is needed on a grand scale. The rehab hospital here is one of the best for my injury, so Harker Heights is where I now call home—the first one I've slept in for more than a month straight during most of my adult life. My superiors set everything up for me. I've got a handicapped accessible home, the van you saw, and it's close enough to Fort Hood." It took her less than twenty minutes to reach the base where, with her extremely high government clearance, she had access to almost every inch of the place.

"That's great . . . I mean, of all the places you could have ended up, I'm glad it was here."

When they reached her van, Haven pulled out her keys and activated the remote that would unlock the door and bring the lift out and down for her. While they waited for it, Frisco stuffed his hands into the front pockets of his pants and rocked back and forth on his feet. "So, when can I see you again? I'd like to take you out to dinner or something . . . you know, on a date."

If she'd been standing, she would've been knocked off her feet. She gaped at him, trying to make sure she'd heard him correctly. "What do you mean 'a date'?"

"A date." He shrugged his shoulders and grinned. "You know—a guy like me, with a really hot woman, like you, who turns him on, going out somewhere that has waiters, wine glasses, and china. They order from leather-covered menus, and the whole time, he's wondering what his chances of getting a goodnight kiss are. That kind of date."

Frowning, Haven shook her head. "I don't think that's a good idea, Frisco."

His eyes narrowed. "Why not? Is there someone else?"

"No, there's no one else." She should have lied and said there was, but it was too late now. God, what she wouldn't give to be her old self again. She would've loved to see where the attraction she felt for him would lead. "I don't go out much—it's a bit of a hassle with the chair and all. Besides, you should be with someone who can keep up with you and do fun things. There's not much fun I can have in a wheelchair."

Rotating the right wheel forward and the left wheel back, Haven spun around and then backed onto the platform, locking herself in. But before she could hit the control to raise it, Frisco put his right foot on the edge of the platform and his hands on the armrests of the chair on either side of her. When she glanced up in surprise, she found him glaring at her, bending down so they were face-to-face. And, damn, he was pissed. His voice dropped low, sending an unwanted chill down her spine. "Do you really think I'm so shallow that this chair bothers me? I'm attracted to *you*, Haven, not whether or not you're standing on two feet. I can handle you being in a chair."

Anger boiled within her. She pushed on his arms, but they wouldn't budge. "Don't you get it? I don't want you to have to *handle* anything. I'm not the woman I used to be, Frisco. I'll never be her again."

"So what? I didn't know that woman beyond the three or four minutes she was begging me to fucking leave her to die. I don't *want* to know that woman. You, right here, right now, are the woman I'm attracted to. The one I'm asking out. The one I want to get to know better."

"I don't need your pity, Frisco."

He huffed harshly and stood erect again. "Is that why you think I'm asking you out? Because I pity you? That's rich. That's fucking rich. Give me a little credit, will you? I'm not the type of guy who asks a woman out because I feel sorry for her. I ask her out because I'm attracted to her. Because I want to spend time with her, learning everything about her.

"Sure, I've had one-night-stands—I'm a guy after all—but I've never led a woman to believe there was something more. Trust me, my interest in you extends beyond a one-night-stand and the last fucking thing I'd do is pity you."

He thrust a hand through his hair and scoffed. "Jesus. All this time I've been carrying around these guilty feelings I might've made your injury worse. At first I thought that's why I couldn't get you out of my head. But when I saw you today, I knew it wasn't guilt that had me dreaming of you at night, it was this intense attraction I felt toward you. But whether or not I made the injury worse shouldn't matter. Do you know why?" He didn't pause to let her answer. "Because you're still alive, and I think someone who works for one of the baddest agencies on the damn planet should be tough enough to get past any curveball life throws at them. The alternative would mean I'd never have the chance to see you again, and up until five minutes ago, that would've really sucked.

"I hope you track down whoever's got that nuke. If you need help with trying to figure it out, call me —I'm sure you can find my number—but don't worry, I won't ask you out again, because you're not the kick-ass woman I thought you were. You're still feeling sorry for yourself . . . and that . . . *that's* what I pity."

Turning on his heel, he stormed over to his car, gave her one final furious glance, then shook his head and climbed into the driver's seat. He floored the accelerator and, with a screech of tires, headed for the exit. Within seconds he was on the main street and out of sight. Haven's heart clenched, as she tried to convince herself turning him down was for the best. But if that was the case, then why were unwelcome tears rolling down her cheeks?

CHAPTER 11

Avery! Where the hell is that thing with the doohickies?" Haven sorted through the stack of files sitting on her desk for the umpteenth time as she bellowed for her assistant. Avery Knapp had been a godsend these past months. The former CIA-turned-Deimos operative, who'd gotten her nursing degree after retiring from the agency fifteen years ago, had been the ideal person to help Haven recover from the shooting. The woman's smooth skin and toned physique belied her age, making her appear far younger than her fifty-five years. In addition to being able to render care as needed, and doing most of the cooking and housecleaning, with her high-security clearance, the woman could also be fully trusted with all the classified information that filled Haven's office. To give them both solitude when needed, a small guest house had been built for Avery in the backyard of the three-acre property that was surrounded by a high-tech security fence, complete with an electronic, retractable gate for the driveway. While both women were no longer field operatives, it didn't mean someone from their past might not come gunning for them one day.

The petite, platinum-haired woman strode into the room, opened the bottom drawer of the filing cabinet closest to the door, and pulled out a yellow folder before handing it to Haven. "That *thing* with said d*oohickies* in it. You know, it's a little ridiculous I understand your filing system better than you do."

Haven huffed as she rolled back over to the massive computer setup that covered an entire wall. "I would have found it eventually."

"Uh-huh. Want to talk about it?"

"Talk about what?"

Avery crossed her arms and leaned against the door frame. "Whatever's had your panties in a twist since you got home. You haven't been this surly in months."

Ignoring the other woman—Haven had no desire to discuss what a bitch she'd been to Frisco with anyone—she flipped through the still photos from the night she'd been shot. Not that she didn't have them memorized after studying them over and over again, hoping someone she'd missed all those other times would jump out at her.

A minute or two passed before Avery sighed and pushed off the jamb. "Fine. Don't talk to me about it. Dinner will be ready in an hour."

Haven was glad when she was finally alone again. Part of her felt like a heel for how she'd treated Frisco, while the other part of her was angry at him for putting her in that position. She didn't need his pity or guilt or whatever it was. If he wanted to be friends, she could handle that, but anything beyond that wasn't going to happen. Haven wasn't even sure if she could have sex with a man anymore and enjoy it. The only way to find out was to do it, but she'd be mortified if things sucked. She'd rather continue to wonder instead of risking knowing for sure if she was less than a responsive woman. She'd always enjoyed sex, but now she doubted she could relax enough with a man for it to be pleasurable. Her mind would be filled with insecurities she hadn't had since she was a teenager with her first boyfriend.

The *click, click, click* of toenails tapping against the wooden floors in the hallway announced Haven was about to have another visitor—this one she could deal with. Avery's golden retriever/border collie mix padded into the room. She plopped her furry butt next to the wheelchair and laid her head on Haven's knee with a sigh.

Unable to resist, Haven lifted her hand and stroked the dog's thick, reddish coat. "Hey, Roxie-girl. Why can't everyone be like you? Mum except for the occasional 'woof' to make me laugh."

As if she'd been cued, Roxie let out a soft *woof*, which brought a smile to Haven's face. "See, that's what I mean."

One thing she'd always wanted growing up was a dog—she loved them. But money had been tight for her mom, who'd raised her two daughters without help from anyone. Then, just after things had improved dramatically for them, when her mom had received a well-deserved promotion and raise after working for the same advertising company for years, it all fell apart at the hands of al Qaeda terrorists. What was supposed to have been a celebratory vacation in Madrid was cut short when ten explosions rocked the Cercanías commuter train system in the middle of rush hour. When the smoke had cleared, Haven had found herself in the hospital with a severe concussion and other non-life-threatening injuries. One hundred ninety-two people were killed, and over 2000 injured. It took four agonizing days for her to receive confirmation her mother and sister were among the dead. On day five, when she was being discharged, an American stranger had walked into her room and, once again, her life was changed forever.

Her cell phone rang, shoving the thoughts about her family, the day she lost them, sex, and the hunky guy she was attracted to, but who now hated her, from her mind. Checking the screen, she was glad to see it was Kenny. She pushed the connect button and made sure her voice sounded cheerful. Her friend was dealing with his own guilty feelings and flashbacks to India—he didn't need her to be a downer and add to them. "Hey, kiddo. What's up?"

"You're only two years older than me, you know."

"Yeah, but you'll always be like a kid brother to me, so I get to call you 'kiddo.' What's up?" she repeated.

The sound of typing came over the line. "I'm sending you some new intel and links. Looks like our mysterious Mr. Smith has decided to pop back up on the Dark Web and is interested in arranging a new meet with Preston Ward."

"What? Hang on." Sitting up straighter in her chair,

Haven put the cell phone on speaker, so she had her hands free. She signed into her secure email account and found the message had already been delivered. She opened it and downloaded the attachment, which was fifteen pages long. In the meantime, she clicked on the first link he'd supplied. Her eyes scanned the chat thread. "Holy shit! Does Gene know this?"

"Just came from his office—he's having a script made up for me to work with. I'll probably start chatting with this bastard sometime tomorrow morning. As soon as I arrange to meet Mr. Smith, Carter and Jordyn will escort me. They're on their way back from Africa and will be here tomorrow night."

"You think it'll be that easy to set up a meeting?"

"No, but you know better than I do terrorists don't do things the way we expect them to, so Mr. McDaniel wants us ready to go at the drop of a hat."

Her chest felt tight at the reminder she was no longer a field operator. If it weren't for the damn wheelchair she'd have been assigned to the mission as well. Her funk was returning, and she didn't want Kenny to worry. "Let me dig into this stuff and see if I spot anything that might help."

There was a long pause on the other end of the

line. When he spoke again, his tone had softened. "Hey, are you doing okay? I mean, really okay?"

"Of course. I'm fine," she responded with false cheer. "I'll talk to you later. Bye."

After disconnecting the call, Haven began stroking Roxie's fur again as she sent the intel to her printer. Her window of opportunity for figuring out who she'd spotted at the wedding just before the explosion had just become smaller. Whoever it was, Haven had a bad feeling about him, which was getting worse each day.

Lying on his back, at an incline, Frisco used his lower limbs and abdominal muscles to push the loaded leg press upward. He may not be able to do exercises for his arms, shoulders, and back at the moment, beyond stretching and range of motion, but there was still plenty he could do. The indoor gym was filled due to the inclement weather that'd blown in, dumping over four inches of rain in a few short hours. A bunch of Deltas were working out around Frisco, but as far as anyone else in the place knew, they were regular soldiers with normal jobs on the base. If you weren't Delta, you didn't get to know who was on the teams.

It had been three days since he'd had lunch with Haven, and he was still pissed. Did she really think he was so shallow he'd be turned off by her disability? For a few moments there, while he'd been holding her hand, talking about the teammates he'd lost, he'd gotten the impression she'd been showing a side of herself very few people had ever seen. It really sucked that the only woman he'd ever met, who had him thinking about things he'd easily done without—a wife, kids, a dog, and a house with a white picket fence—didn't feel the same way.

"Are you going to bend your knees again, or just hold the weight up for the rest of the damn day?" Fletch stood above Frisco, his brow raised in question.

Turning the handles to lock the platform in place, Frisco lowered his legs, got to his feet, and wiped his sweat from the machine's back pad. "Sorry. Spaced out for a moment."

"It wouldn't have to do with a hot-looking brunette you ran into the other day, would it?" the other man asked as he took the spot Frisco had just vacated.

He glared at his two teammates Trigger and Oz,

who were doing bicep curls, with free weights a few feet away. "You two have big fucking mouths."

It had been a stupid thing to do, meet his buddies for drinks the other night when he was still seething—and heartbroken—over his blowup with Haven. He should have kept his own big mouth shut.

Trigger dropped his heavy curl bar to the mat he was standing on, then shrugged, but didn't offer an apology. These men were Frisco's brothers, and they gave each other shit all the time. But they also covered everyone else's six, on and off the battle-fields. They'd all known he was still bothered by that night in India, but it was something he had to work out for himself. Each one of the Deltas had lost someone in combat. Since 9/11, it was hard to find someone in the military who hadn't. Many of them also knew what it was like to have a teammate permanently disabled and/or disfigured by bombs, RPGs, bullets, or other forms of destruction, but each dealt with it in his or her own way. However, Frisco's problem was he couldn't get past the attrac-tion he felt toward Haven, something he'd never experienced before with a teammate. While his current team was all men, he'd had women in his squads before going into Special Forces. Technically, Haven wasn't their teammate, but they defended the same flag and constitution, bound together by love of, and loyalty to, their country. They'd been on the same mission to take down a terrorist hell bent on destroying the American way of life, therefore, for a brief period of time, she'd been one of them. And one thing the Deltas did better than anyone was take care of their own.

Grabbing his towel, Frisco wiped his face, then guzzled half the water in his bottle. He was just about to head toward the treadmills when a bunch of cell phones chirped or buzzed with an incoming text. He glanced around and saw members from three different Delta teams check their devices. *Shit, that's not good.* Frisco looked at the text on his phone.

Mission alert. Briefing room #1. 1130 hours.

Damn it. Frisco wasn't medically cleared, yet, so he was probably going to have to sit this one out, but he still had to go to the meeting. They all hated to be left behind when missions rolled around, but it was even worse if someone got hurt or killed during it. That whole "what if" game came into play again. *What if I'd gone on the mission? Would that have altered the universe enough to have made a difference? Or would that teammate still have gotten injured or lost his life?*

A few of the Deltas headed for the showers, while the others finished their last sets first. They had about forty-five minutes to clean up, grab lunch on the way, and hightail it to the briefing room on the other side of the base. Frisco decided to leave his run until later since he was usually on the treadmill for about an hour. Downing the last of the water, he tossed the empty bottle in the recycle bin on his way to the locker room, pushing thoughts of Haven from his mind. He had to get over her somehow.

Three quarters of an hour later, the larger of two briefing rooms was filled. Deltas from three different teams sat in rows of chairs that faced the podium or stood in the aisles as they chatted. Thanks to a phone call from his mother, giving him an update on his dad's latest stress test, Frisco had been one of the last people in and ended up taking a seat at the back of the room. After a mild heart attack last year, the elder Ingram had been doing what he could to keep his cholesterol and blood pressure within normal limits. He'd started eating healthier and exercising more, which had resulted in a twenty-pound weight loss. He'd also retired, after twenty-five years, from his stressful job as an air traffic controller at San Francisco International Airport, and had taken a position with the Oakland Aviation Museum in the East Bay Area, much to his family's relief.

"Attention!"

Ghost's barked command had everyone on their feet, arms at their sides, eyes straight ahead, facing the podium. From the doorway near the front of the room, their colonel walked in. "As you were. Let's get started."

Almost as one, the men sat as the colonel stood behind the podium and looked out over those under his command. Seated to his right were the ranking officers of each team. He cleared his throat to make sure he had everyone's attention, not that he needed to do so; everyone was already silent, waiting for him to speak. "All right—for once, as I'm sure Captain Bryson is happy to hear, the feds and military are sharing intel before the shit gets too deep. The elusive 'Mr. Smith' from that clusterfuck in Mumbai a few months ago has made an appearance on the Dark Web, looking to arrange a new meeting with the person he believes has the nuke codes. Apparently, he's chosen Mexico, just over the Texas border, as the location for the deal to go down, and you'll be backing up the agents from Deimos. We don't have complete details as of yet. After India, he's being even more cautious, not giving the time and location until the last minute. The only reason we have Mexico is he has no idea where the seller is coming from and how long it will take him to get there. I'll let Agent Caldwell fill you in with what her agency knows. Agent Caldwell?"

Frisco's jaw dropped as he strained to see over everyone's head. What were the chances there was more than one Agent Caldwell in Deimos? Unfortunately, because of her wheelchair, he was too far back and couldn't see more than a flash of her brunette hair as she positioned herself in front of the elevated podium. But it'd been just enough for him to confirm it was Haven.

"Thank you, Colonel. I apologize to those in the back who can't see me, but I'll try to speak loud enough to be heard." Captain Bryson and another officer stood and began handing out orange folders —the color signifying the information inside was extremely classified and was not allowed to leave the building. When the mission was complete, the pages within would be shredded and then incinerated. As the two men made sure every Delta member present got one, Haven continued. "The communications team at Deimos intercepted several attempts made by Mr. Smith to contact Preston Ward on Monday. For those of you who weren't on the mission in Mumbai, that's a persona the agency has cultivated over the years. Preston's a reclusive computer hacker with a penchant for trading anything that piques his interest for cash or intel. We've made sure he's on the watch lists for the FBI and CIA, as well as agencies around the globe, but his travel hasn't been restricted. He's also an expert at covering his tracks and has never been caught . . . obviously. It's kind of hard to capture and hang a person who only exists on paper, unless he's Flat Stanley." Her sarcastic joke about the popular figure from an educational project that'd spread around the world was met with a bunch of chuckles, mostly from men who had kids.

"Our computer specialist who portrayed Preston Ward in Mumbai is on his way to Texas with the two agents assigned to him. It could be a few days, a week, or a month before he's contacted with the time and place for the exchange of $10 million for the codes to a nuke that was stolen from Russia in 1995. The US and its allies have been searching for it ever since. It's one of dozens that went missing around that time, however, this one left a trail after it was taken. During the getaway, the codes were separated from the device, but we assume it was done on purpose with the intent of later reuniting the two. We know for a fact that never happened." In other words, the codes were probably secured somewhere within the United States, having been recovered before now.

"The device is roughly the size of an extra-large suitcase, and the codes were on a software protection dongle. For those who don't know what that is, it's the predecessor to DRM—digital rights management—used in gaming systems and digital media, like e-books. The hardware key is difficult to crack, and when it comes to a nuclear device, I highly doubt you want to take a chance it'll go off if the wrong code is entered.

"Now, when MI6 intercepted three known suspects in London, two months after the theft, they were no longer in possession of the nuke. There was a gun battle, and all three were shot and killed along with an agent and a police officer. We have no idea where the device has been all this time. Approximately eleven months ago, Mr. Smith showed up on the Dark Web searching for the codes. As I'm sure everyone here knows, his first attempt to get them was a failure—whether or not he was involved in the disaster in Mumbai is still up for debate.

"Are there any questions?"

Frisco had a bunch of them, but none were appropriate at the moment. They had nothing to do with the mission and everything to do with the beautiful spy at the front of the room. The spy he still hadn't been able to see completely. Several men raised their hands, and Haven answered their inquiries as best she could. There were quite a few holes in the mission, as it stood now, but hopefully they'd be filled in as more intel came in and the meeting between Mr. Smith and Preston Ward was scheduled.

When there were no more questions, the colonel addressed his men. "Another briefing will take place tomorrow at 0800. Captain Bryson will be the lead on this detail. First Sergeant Ingram, where are you?"

Surprised at being singled out, Frisco jumped to his feet and stood at attention. "Here, sir."

"Stay behind and see me. The rest of you are dismissed."

As the teams filed out the two available doors, Frisco weaved his way through the small crowd. When he finally reached the front of the room, the colonel was talking to Haven. His cock twitched at the sight of her. *Damn it, not now!*

Dressed in a professional, black pant suit, with a royal blue blouse, Haven had her hair up in a pony-tail, just like the last two times he'd seen her. He yearned to pull on the elastic band, setting the strands free so he could run his fingers through them. In practically every fantasy he'd had, her hair was down, framing her face, as it had been during that fateful mission.

Her gaze met his, and he could tell she was just as surprised as he was the colonel had requested to see him. A slight blush stained her cheeks, causing his ire from the other day to lessen under his reemerging lust for her.

Standing nearby, Ghost loudly cleared his throat, catching Frisco's attention with the clear but unspoken reprimand. Giving himself a mental shake, he stood at attention and addressed the colonel. "Sorry, sir. You wanted to see me?"

"At ease, Frisco." The use of the moniker, instead of his rank and last name, had indicated this was going to be a casual conversation. Frisco relaxed as the colonel continued. "I understand you and Agent Caldwell met in Mumbai."

Uh-oh.

CHAPTER 12

HAVEN'S STOMACH STARTED DOING BACKFLIPS. SHE'D already known the colonel was going to assign one of his men as a go-between for her and his teams, but with approximately thirty soldiers in the room, she'd figured she had around a 3.3% chance of being paired with Frisco. Maybe she should go buy a lottery ticket.

It was clear Frisco knew his supervisor's intent as he responded, "Yes, sir, we did." There was no need to explain further since the man was undoubtedly aware of everything that'd happened during and immediately after that mission—but did that include the death wish Haven had asked for?

"Good. Since you'll be on light duty for a few more weeks, I'm assigning you to Agent Caldwell.

Make sure she has access to anything she needs from us. From what she's told me, it's easier to work out of her house where she has secure access to her agency." He turned to Haven. "Agent Caldwell, thank you for opening your home to us. If you need anything, just let Frisco know, and we'll take care of it."

"Thank you, Colonel. I appreciate that." Haven's smile was forced, but either the colonel didn't notice or was polite enough to ignore it.

"If you'll excuse me, I have another meeting on my agenda."

"Certainly."

As the older man left the room, Ghost held out his hand to Haven. "We haven't had the pleasure yet, ma'am. I'm Captain Bryson, but you can call me Keane or Ghost, preferably the latter."

Laughing, Haven shook his hand. "Ghost it is, as long as you don't call me ma'am. Haven will do."

"Okay, Haven, if you need anything and Frisco is off duty, you can call me anytime, and I'll get it done."

He handed her a small card with his name and cell number on it. She slid it into a pouch attached to the right arm of the chair. "Thank you."

Turning, he addressed Frisco. "Let me know if

you need anything delivered to Haven's house—maps, comms, whatever."

"I will."

Whatever unspoken message the two men had as their eyes met, Haven couldn't decipher. She had no idea if Frisco's superior knew the details of his visit to her in the rehab hospital or their run-in at physical therapy a few days ago. After Ghost left them alone, silence filled the air. It took a moment for Haven to get the courage to look Frisco in the eye. "It seems I keep apologizing to you, but I'm sorry about the other day." When he didn't say anything, she continued. "I—you just caught me off guard . . . I . . . do you mind sitting for a minute so I don't get a crick in my neck? There must be a height requirement for Deltas; you all seem awfully tall."

Her attempt at easing the tension between them didn't seem to work, but at least he did take a seat in the front row. He crossed his arms and waited for her to resume the apology he rightfully deserved.

"Thanks. Listen, I had no idea you were going to be assigned to me and I can't figure out any way to change it. You have to follow orders, and if I request someone else, it will probably be an issue with your superiors too, and I don't want that to happen. So,

I'm willing to work with you—hell, I'm willing to be friends with you—but that's as far as it can go, Frisco. I'm dealing with way too much to even consider dating someone. I don't even *know* how to date someone who's not a target or a cover—it's been far too long. Can we just be—friends?"

She prayed he hadn't heard that her question was filled with a combination of desperation and hope. She'd been thinking about him non-stop the past few days and couldn't deny she was attracted to him. But it also went beyond that. She'd had fun joking around and conversing with him the other day, even if most of it was work related. Maybe her loneliness was getting to her. Avery, Kenny, Carter, and Jordyn were the only people she talked to nowadays. When she'd been a field operative, her covers and traveling had required her to talk to all sorts of people, even though she would classify herself as a loner. Acquaintances were fine. The occasional one-night or two-night stand? Those were okay too. But anything beyond that, she'd rather be alone.

She hadn't always been that way—she'd had plenty of friends in high school and college. When her mom and sister were alive, they were always laughing and talking about all sorts of things.

Window shopping was a favorite pastime for the three women. They loved going into boutiques and trying on all the clothes they couldn't afford. It was ironic Haven now owned clothes from the hottest designers in the world. She'd needed them for her cover, and the US government had paid for them. Not that she'd been wearing many of them anymore. There were boxes of high-fashion dresses, shoes, outfits, and accessories in the garage of her new home. Everything, except for the furniture, had been packed up from her apartments in Los Angeles, New York, Washington D.C., and London and shipped to her. She still hadn't gone through any of the boxes.

It surprised her she now hated the silence and alone time she'd craved these past thirteen years since she'd become a field operative for the most secret agency in the United States. She wouldn't admit it, but she liked when Avery insisted on making conversation with her. She found herself looking forward to Kenny's phone calls to check on her. She'd also grown closer to Jordyn and Carter. They tried to stop in whenever they could, and called when they couldn't. But then, at night, after Avery and Roxie returned to the guest house, the deafening silence was starting to drive Haven crazy.

She'd like to have people she could call friends again —she'd been without them for far too long—and she'd like to start with Frisco. Maybe someday, when she was finally able to do without the damn wheelchair, they could explore a romantic relationship.

Frisco took a deep breath and let it out. "Friends, huh? I think I can handle that." A smile spread across his handsome face. "This doesn't mean I'm not going to try and convince you we can be more— after all, I'm a guy, and you're an incredibly beautiful woman I'm attracted to—but I promise not to push. If I overstep my bounds and make you uncomfortable, just tell me, and I'll back off. Deal?"

She pretended to give it a long, deep thought, before she thrust out her hand. "Deal."

"Thanks, man." Frisco shook hands with the young analyst from Fort Hood's Intelligence Department who'd dropped off some updated maps and satellite photos of several areas everyone thought Mr. Smith might use for the exchange. He then escorted the soldier out the front door of Haven's house. She'd cleared off an area on the rarely-used wooden desk in her office, for her new partner. Apparently, she spent most of her time in front of the large computer and monitoring system that occupied one whole wall on the opposite side of the room. A contractor had combined two standard-sized bedrooms to create one large area for her to work in. Frisco had actually been surprised she'd let him into her inner sanctum instead of banishing him to the dining room or kitchen table.

With help from the intel guy, he'd spent the past hour pinning the maps and photos to the remaining three walls of the office. More monitors and other equipment would be arriving tomorrow. When they got the location for the exchange, they'd need to hack into any camera systems in the area. There'd also be live-action feeds coming from the Deltas' body cams.

As he strolled back to the office, her assistant's dog, Roxie, followed him. She was extremely friendly and had taken to him immediately. Frisco missed having a dog around. He'd grown up with several, but never knowing when he'd be sent out on a mission or how long he'd be gone wasn't conducive to owning one.

He eyed the kitchen as he passed. It was designed for a handicapped person, as well as an able-bodied one. Some of the cabinets and counter-tops were low enough for Haven to use, and she would be able to roll close to the sink and cook-top, which had an open space underneath for her legs. The refrigerator/freezer was a side-by-side one, so she could access both. The bathroom was also retro-fitted to accommodate her chair. The hallways and doorways were wider than normal, and furniture was placed so she could easily maneuver around each piece. Out back, there was a lap pool where she could strengthen her leg muscles, a patio with plenty of shade to relax on, and the guest house for her assistant.

Avery Knapp was an interesting woman. To most people, she probably looked like exactly what she portrayed—a woman in her midfifties, with a nursing degree, who was an assistant/compan-ion/housekeeper. While she was all that, Frisco saw more. When you were in black-ops, it was much easier to spot those who were also part of the community. It was in the way they greeted you, sized you up, and analyzed whether or not you were a threat, all within a second or two. She'd eyed him shrewdly when Haven had introduced them the other day, and he'd received her approval after inter-rogating him, in a roundabout way, for several minutes. If he hadn't taken a course on the subtleties of questioning a target without revealing he was on your radar, Frisco may have thought she was just being friendly. He had no doubt, if he hadn't passed her test, he would have been out on his ass. He also hadn't missed the fact the petite woman was in better physical condition than most people half her age—and she was packing. The tell-tale signs of a concealed weapon at the small of her back had almost been undetectable under her loose fitting T-shirt and jeans.

After they'd left the base the day he'd been assigned to her, Frisco had followed Haven to her home and was impressed by the security measures in place. The property was surrounded by a tall, stone and iron fence. While that was common in the surrounding neighborhood of expensive homes, what made this one special was the barbed wire that ran along the top of it, not high enough to be seen, but enough to rip someone's hands to shreds if they tried to scale the wall. There were also sensors that were parallel to the wire on either side of it, that would signal the occupants of the house that someone was trying to gain entry. According to Haven, a certain amount of weight had to be applied so the alarm wouldn't go off thanks to birds or squirrels. It wasn't entirely fool-proof, but combined with other safeguards around the property and two houses, they'd give Haven and Avery time to defend themselves. While an attack was unlikely, given who they were employed by, all precautions had to be taken. Frisco had also learned that Haven's van was actually made of bulletproof panels and glass. Avery's SUV was too.

Entering the large office, Frisco strode over to the desk and sat down in front of his computer. Roxie seemed undecided about who to go to, one of her constant companions or the newcomer who scratched her ears until she moaned, so she flopped down on the floor between them with a heavy sigh. Such decisions had to be exhausting for the active canine.

Like she'd been for the past two hours, Haven was deep into something on her computer, searching the Dark Web. Frisco studied her while she scanned whatever was on her screen. He was pretty good with modern technology, and had even been on the seedier side of the internet a few times, but he usually left that to those who really knew what they were doing. Besides, he was more inter-ested in the woman than what she was reading. He was sure if it was important, she'd let him know.

The fact that she still couldn't remember the mystery man she'd seen at the wedding was driving her nuts. When she wasn't on the computer, she was pouring through the photos and videos from that night.

They'd fallen into a comfortable routine the past week. The first few days, he'd arrived at 0800 hours, and they spent hours guessing at possible sites the suspect might choose. The three Delta teams had been dispatched to the Texas cities of Del Rio, Laredo, and McAllen, all on the Mexican border. It would be faster for at least one of the teams to get to the target destination from any of those locations. Carter and Jordyn had Reardon holed up in a safe house in San Antonio. The geek had his own setup there to access the Dark Web, but there hadn't been any contact from the elusive Mr. Smith since he'd told "Preston Ward" the meeting would be somewhere south of the border.

After Frisco had fallen asleep in the executive desk chair he was currently sitting in one evening, Haven had taken pity on him and told him to crash on the couch, due to the lack of a guest bed. Since then, he'd slept there every night, having brought some clothes and things in a duffel bag from his apartment. While he'd have preferred to sleep in

Haven's bed, the couch was actually pretty comfortable.

Frisco glanced at the clock on his computer screen. "Hey, it's six o'clock. Since Avery has the night off to visit with her niece, what do you say we order a pizza?"

"Sounds good. Just no anchovies." Haven hadn't taken her eyes off the screen as she spoke.

Sighing, he stood, strode over to her console, and rested his ass against the desk top. "Haven?"

When she didn't look at him, he cupped her chin and turned her head toward him. Her eyes narrowed. "What?"

"You've been at it for hours—for days. You need to take a break. I'll order a pizza, we can find a movie on TV and act like normal people for a change. You can't work yourself into the ground." The only breaks he knew she'd been taking were to sleep, shower, eat, and go to therapy. They'd coordinated their appointments so they could ride over together in her van.

Frisco couldn't stop himself from brushing his thumb back and forth over her soft cheek as he stared into her cognac-colored eyes. "C'mon, whatta ya say? I'll even let you choose the movie."

He thought for sure she was going to turn him

down, as she'd done several times this week when he'd tried to get her to relax and unwind, but this time she surprised him. She opened a drawer on the other side of her chair, withdrew a takeout menu, and handed it to him. "Okay. But I want Chinese instead of pizza. I'm in the mood for General Tso's shrimp and pork fried rice."

Grinning, he opened the menu and scanned the fifty or so choices. "What else is good besides that? We can share."

"Who said anything about sharing?" she asked with a smirk. "I don't share my General Tso's shrimp with anybody."

"Hmm . . . not even with someone ordering Szechuan beef?"

"Mmm. You drive a hard bargain. I might be persuaded to swap a few bites, *if* . . . you let me have your fortune cookie."

His brow raised at her playfulness. He'd been flirting with her all week, and while she hadn't said he was overstepping the boundaries between them, she also hadn't flirted back . . . until tonight. "Tell you what, I'll order extra."

Haven pushed on the wheels of her chair and rolled backward. "Great. While you call it in, I'm going to hop in the shower."

"I can scrub your back if you want."

The blush he loved so much was back, staining her cheeks. "I got it covered, stud. Thanks anyway."

His laughter followed her out the door. Maybe he was finally growing on her. *Awesome.*

CHAPTER 13

AFTER STRIPPING OFF HER CLOTHES, HAVEN transferred herself to the sturdy, plastic seat in the extra-large, handicapped shower with the spray already on full blast. Usually, she would let the water warm up, but didn't wait this time. A little cold water would temper her burning cheeks and raging hormones. All week, she'd kept herself in check and made sure she didn't lead Frisco on by responding to his flirting. But tonight, her control had flown out the window when he'd cupped her chin, and those wicked eyes had bored into her. Her jaw and cheek still tingled from where he'd rubbed his thumb back and forth, and that feeling had shot straight to her core. It had taken all her strength to propel her chair out of the room. If she wasn't careful, the man would work his way under her skin more than he'd already done.

Once her hair was soaked, she grabbed a bottle of her favorite shampoo, which smelled like roses, from the shower's low shelf. Actually, it'd been her sister's favorite, and Haven liked to use it to bring back happy memories that weren't marred by terrorists determined to kill anyone who didn't pray to the same deity they did. But this time as she worked the scented lather into her strands of hair, her mind conjured up the man who was currently ordering their dinner.

If this were another time and place, she'd have already invited Frisco into her bed, of that she was certain. But she saw the way he looked at her sometimes when he didn't think she was paying attention, and that usually stopped her in her tracks. He wanted her in his bed—he'd made no attempt to hide that fact—but she got the feeling he wanted more than that . . . more than what she could give him. Haven had no idea how to be herself around a man like him. For thirteen years, up to the point she was shot, she'd played a role, even if she wasn't on a mission. She always had to be "on," like an actor staying in character during an entire filming schedule. The only place she could relax and be herself was alone, behind closed doors. But Lucas "Frisco" Ingram was slowly working his way past the defensive walls she'd built around her heart, and it scared her shitless. She was so afraid that if he got to know the real Haven, the one she kept hidden from the rest of the world, he'd be disappointed and walk away. She couldn't handle any more loss in her life—there had been far too much already.

But the way he made her feel, just by roaming his gaze over her from head to toe like he wanted to devour her, was weakening her defenses. Each day, she became more attracted to him and often found herself daydreaming about what it would be like for him to kiss her, strip her naked, and bring her to orgasm after orgasm. Her long-dormant sexual desires were rising to the surface again, and when Frisco was in the room they were ready to spill over, taking her doubts with them.

Once more, she felt a stirring between her legs. "Damn it," she muttered to herself as she rinsed the shampoo from her hair. "Thinking about him all day long is not helping."

After several moments of hesitation, Haven rolled her eyes and reached for the bottle of body oil she kept on the shower's shelf. "Might as well figure out if everything's working without an audience."

Pouring some of the oil onto her fingers, she spread her legs a little wider. Leaning on the chair-back, she closed her eyes and conjured up Frisco. Every day in therapy she was treated to a delicious sight when he took his shirt off so the therapists could get at his shoulders and neck. He was sculpted perfection under his cotton T-shirts, and she wondered what the loose pants and shorts he wore hid, certain she wouldn't be disappointed.

Trailing her hand down her abdomen, she paused for a moment, before allowing her fingers to brush across her clit. She gasped at the contact, even though she'd been expecting it. She did it again as, in her mind, Frisco went down on his knees in front of her. He kissed the inside of her thighs as he worked his way up to her pussy. While she'd recently begun trimming herself down there, she really wanted to go get waxed again. Up until the day she was shot, she'd always kept herself bare, sans a small patch above her clit.

As Frisco did wicked things to her in her daydream, her fingers began to work their magic. Dipping them inside her tight pussy, she drove herself higher. Haven forced herself to push everything else from her mind except what her fantasy lover was doing to her. Lifting her other hand to her breasts, she rolled the taut peaks between her fingers, pulling on them. Her breathing increased as she found her clit again and rubbed furiously. Frisco was spreading her wider and eating her like she was the sweetest fruit on Earth.

That's it, baby. Give me more. Give me all of it.

Harder. Faster. Demanding everything she had. Refusing to take a small sample. He wanted everything she had to offer.

Cum for me, Haven. Cum for me, now!

Haven shattered around her fingers. Her body shook with abandon as her other hand shot out to grab the shower's safety bar. She bit her bottom lip to keep from crying out as wave after wave of pleasure coursed through her. It'd been so long since she'd climaxed, she thought she'd pass out from the intensity. Her fingers drew out the orgasm as long as possible, before she began to float back to reality. Behind her closed eyelids, she saw Frisco looking at her from between her legs. His chin was covered with the evidence of her release as he grinned with satisfaction. *"That's my girl. Ready for round two?"*

WITH HAVEN CURLED UP TO HIS RIGHT, HER HEAD

resting on the pillow in his lap, and Roxie, to his left, snuggled against him, Frisco couldn't get up. He was thanking his lucky stars the remote was in reach and he didn't need to use the bathroom; he didn't want to disturb either of them. His hands had stroked both of them—Haven's chestnut hair, which was still slightly damp, and Roxie's reddish-blonde fur—long after they'd started to snore softly in tandem. Picking up the remote from the other side of the dog, he lowered the volume of the TV as the last of the credits for *Skyfall* ended and *Spectre* began. He'd been surprised at Haven's choice of the James Bond films. Then again, she used to do a lot of things that could've been used for a series franchise about a female spy . . . if the public ever found out about it, which probably wouldn't happen.

Frisco adjusted his hips the best he could without waking the two sleepers. His dick had been hard for the past half hour—more so than earlier when he'd been thinking about Haven naked in the shower. With her hand tucked under his thigh, her fingers were curved around his leg, stopping just below his sweatpants-covered balls. He knew it was unintentional on her part—she'd been out like a light when it'd happened—but still it was driving him crazy. Every once in a while, her fingers twitched or tightened briefly, and he wished they were wrapped around his aching cock instead. If it wasn't for the pillow, he'd be hitting her in the ear with it, and that wasn't the part of her body the damn thing wanted to be in.

He could really get used to this. Not only was he attracted to Haven on a sexual level, he liked being with her. There were a lot of guys he knew who considered their wives or girlfriends to be their best friends, but he never really got it before now. In only a week, he felt more comfortable with her than he'd ever been with another woman in his life. He'd told her all about his family the other night over a cup of coffee and dessert after Avery had gone back to the guest house following dinner. She'd seemed honestly interested in the funny stories that had become part of his family's history over the years. Then she'd listened with sympathy as he'd explained how he'd lost several good friends on the battlefields of Iraq and Afghanistan. While he'd never forget any of them, the one incident that often woke him up in a cold sweat was the one he should have been killed in, too.

It was actually embarrassing why he was still alive and the others were dead. It'd been a year before he'd become an Army Ranger, and almost three years before he'd joined the elite Delta Force. He and his unit had been two days away from going home after a six-month tour. They could almost taste the American air they'd been missing, along with pizza, barbecue, and anything else that didn't come from a mess hall or MRE package. Ten members of his squad had been loading up to leave the confines of Camp Leatherneck for a run to Kandahar, escorting a small convoy of supply trucks. Frisco's intestinal system had been revolting against that morning's breakfast, and he was suffering from a severe case of the farts. The guys he'd been serving with for nearly two years had banished him to another Humvee with some of the newer arrivals to the base, instead of having him stink up their vehicle. With no AC and areas where having open windows was an invitation to get shot in the head, they'd wanted no part of his gastric distress. Laughing, they'd locked him out of the vehicle, telling him to hitch a ride in the other one. His grumbling had been cut short about two miles from camp when the lead Humvee, filled with his best friend and other buddies, ran over a concealed bomb. The explosion had ripped through the bottom of the vehicle, instantly killing everyone on board except the driver, who'd died hours later while in surgery.

Four friends, who'd been through hell and back with him for two tours, were gone in the blink of an eye. Frisco had been beyond devastated, and his superiors had known it. Since he was already rotating home, they'd granted him permission to accompany the bodies of his teammates back to the US for burial. He spent the entire trip aboard a C-130, a military transport plane designed to carry only rows of flag-covered caskets of fallen heroes and their escorts.

After landing at Dover AFB, a solemn, dignified transfer of the remains of the dead followed, before they were transported to whichever part of the country their families had requested. Frisco had stayed with two of his buddies, including his best friend, Joshua "Digger" Riggs, who'd been placed on the commercial flight heading to Columbus, Georgia, near Fort Benning where they'd been stationed at the time. Digger's family had flown in to escort their son and brother home. Frisco had barely gotten through the funerals, and if it wasn't for Digger's father, he may never have gotten on Delta. He could still hear the older man's words after they were the only two still remaining at the grave site.

Retired Army Gunnery Sergeant Michael Riggs grabbed the younger man by the shoulders and made sure he had his attention. Riggs had aged ten years since he'd been notified of his son's death, but he still gave his support to those around him, who were also grieving. "Now, you listen here, Frisco. I know what you're going through—I've been there many times during my tours. You're wondering how the hell to go on after this." He pointed to the still open grave. "This was not your fault. Put the blame where it belongs—with those bastards who planted that bomb. Josh and the others wouldn't want you to give up your dreams for them. I know you both put in for the Rangers with the intent of going all the way to Delta. When you get that call, I want you to go and be the best damn Ranger then Delta the US has ever seen. You do it for him . . . for all of them. I know you won't be able to tell me when you do make it to Delta—notice I didn't say if— but I'll know. And I'll be damn proud of you. So will Josh. Every mission you go on, know they'll have your six." He tapped Frisco's temple and then the left side of his sternum with his finger. "You'll feel them here and here."

Two months later, Frisco had gotten the call to join the 75th Ranger Regiment. After passing the training, he spent two years with them before being selected for Delta Force. With Michael Riggs's words resonating in his mind, there had never been a moment of doubt that he wouldn't complete the rigorous, six-month Operator Training Course.

Two days after graduation, he'd learned that Digger's father was near death after a year-long battle with cancer. Having a week's leave before he was due at Fort Hood, Frisco had flown to Columbus, Georgia. Upon his arrival at the Riggs's family home, he'd been greeted warmly by Digger's mom and three sisters, before walking into the living room where a hospital bed had been set up.

Thinking he'd arrived too late—the older man had been in and out of consciousness for three days —Frisco was surprised when Mr. Riggs's eyes opened and focused on him. Unable to speak, he'd used the little energy he still had to raise his eyebrows. Frisco had nodded in response. "You tell them, I did it, Gunny. I did it for you, them, and every veteran who's ever defended our flag."

A smile had spread across the man's pale and drawn face. Three hours later, surrounded by his family and his son's best friend, Michael Riggs passed away.

CHAPTER 14

Frisco's eyes were shut, but he was still awake. A faint click, barely discernible over the low volume of the TV, had his lids opening in a flash. Roxie had apparently heard the same thing because she lifted her head and stared toward the kitchen. When her tail started thumping softly against the back of the couch, Frisco relaxed again. It had to be Avery since the dog barked for everyone but her and Haven. Rising to her four paws, the retriever-mix hopped down and stretched before trotting over to her mistress as Avery walked into the room on silent feet. She bent down to scratch Roxie's ears and crooned softly, "Hey, sweetheart. Did you miss me?"

From the way the dog groaned and leaned into the caress, while her tail went a mile a minute, it was apparent she did. Avery glanced at the couple on the couch and raised an eyebrow at Frisco. Haven was still out like a light in the same position she'd been in earlier. He'd placed a throw blanket over her to keep her from getting cold in the cotton shorts and tank top she'd put on after her shower.

Avery smiled. "Hmm. I knew the moment I met you, if anyone could break through her defenses, it would be you. You're good for her. That being said, you hurt her, and they'll never find your body. Got it?"

That the petite woman in her fifties was threatening him, a highly trained Delta operative, would have been comical to most people. However, Frisco was sure she'd done her share of damage to enemies of the US and would have no problem taking one down today. He wondered if becoming a nurse was to atone for any deaths by her hand during her prior career. "Duly noted. The last thing I'd ever do is hurt her."

"I know. Just wanted it on record. Come on, Roxie. Let's leave these two lovebirds alone. Have a good night, Frisco."

"You, too, Avery."

After they left for the guest house, Frisco used the remote to turn off the TV. Gently lifting the pillow and Haven's head, he slid out from under them and stood. Tucking his hands under her back and thighs, he lifted and carried her to the master bedroom. He loved the feel of her in his arms, her head resting on his shoulder. Bending over, he grasped the covers of the bed with the hand that was still under her legs and pulled them down, before setting her on the mattress. Drawing the sheet and blanket on top of her, he shut off the bedside lamp she'd left on earlier. He then returned to the living room to throw out the empty plates and cartons from their dinner. Retrieving her wheelchair, he placed it next to the bed where she could reach it.

After staring at Haven's sleeping form for a few more moments, committing it to memory, he was about to head back out to the couch when she moaned. Her head rocked back and forth as she reached up into the air for something he couldn't see. "Noooo! M-Mom . . . Tara . . . I'm sorry . . . so sorry."

Frisco was shocked at her mention of family. He knew she didn't have any now, but from the sound of it, Haven had lost some of them tragically. Her restlessness increased as her legs moved slightly under the covers, but she was still sound asleep. "It's all my fault . . . noooooooo!"

He grabbed her hand, before it could knock over the lamp, and squatted next to the bed. Brushing his other hand across her forehead, he whispered, "Sh. Haven. It's okay. You're safe. It's okay, baby. I'm here."

It took a few moments of reassuring her before she quieted under his touch. Her hands closed around his arm and pulled him closer. It was probably the stupidest idea of his recent past, but Frisco couldn't let her go. Carter's words from months ago, sitting in the restaurant, came back to him. Sometimes what a person wanted, wasn't what they needed. And Haven needed him; there was no way he'd be able to sleep on the couch tonight, knowing that.

Fishing into his pocket, he pulled out his wallet and phone and placed them on her night stand. He'd discarded his socks and sneakers earlier out in the living room. Carefully climbing over Haven, he slipped under the blankets and stretched out beside her on the queen-sized bed, resting his head on the spare pillow. She turned on her side, away from him, clutching his forearm to her chest. Scooting closer, he spooned her, his front torso against her back. He stayed awake until her soft breathing told him she was no longer having the nightmare, then closed his eyes and followed her into slumber.

Haven woke up feeling safe and secure . . . and something poking her in the ass. A heavy weight lay across her waist and slow, steady breaths tickled her neck. She stayed perfectly still as her eyes blinked open. It was hot in the bedroom, but that probably had a lot to do with the hunky guy spooning her in his sleep. The military wristwatch on the arm that was wrapped around her was a dead giveaway. Well, that and the fact she highly doubted anyone would break through the property's high-tech security system just to climb into bed with her and fall asleep —if anything, they'd do it to slit her throat.

As her mind cleared, she remembered him putting a pillow on his lap last night as they watched the movie, encouraging her to lay down and relax. She hadn't thought she'd be able to, since the only time she'd ever relaxed in the past was when she'd been alone, but apparently it had worked. Somehow, Frisco had gotten her to drop her defenses and let him take care of her. What was she going to do about him?

She wanted nothing more than to roll over and wake him up with her lips on his and her hand down his pants. Last night in the shower had proven all her girlie parts were in working order, but masturbating and fucking a man were two different things. He'd already told her he could handle her disability, that he wasn't bothered by it at all, but could she trust he wouldn't regret it later or find her lacking in some way? While her mind still held onto slivers of doubt, her heart told her something else. Frisco was the type of man she'd spent her teen years and early twenties dreaming about—strong, confident, good-looking, smart, gentle—everything the alpha males had been in the romance novels she used to read. But he was so much more than that. He had her daydreaming about a normal life again— one with a future.

"You're thinking too hard," he murmured in a sleepy voice. "I'm not going to jump you, but there's nothing I can do about the morning wood. I'm a guy, remember?"

Oh, she definitely remembered, even without the stiff reminder. "Is there any particular reason you're in my bed?"

"Mm-hmm. I had no choice. You grabbed my arm and flipped me over you after I carried you in here. By the way, you snore."

Haven scoffed. "I do not!"

"Yes, you do, but I'm not complaining. It's cute."

Turning, she faced him, chest to chest, as he adjusted the covers over them. His eyes were still shut as if he didn't want the day to start. When she inhaled, his potent, male scent teased her nose and made her mouth water. She brushed her fingers over his brow, and that made him lift his eyelids, but he remained silent as she gently traced the contours of his face. "What do you see in me?"

His eyes narrowed. "What do you mean?"

"I mean, I don't know who I am anymore. I don't know who I'm supposed to be. I've pretended to be so many different people over the years that I don't know who Haven Caldwell is . . . hell, that's not even my real name."

"I won't ask what it is." He grasped her hand and kissed her fingertips. "You'll tell me someday. But you'll always be Haven to me—not the one before you were hurt, but this one. I like you, baby, a lot—warts and all. Hell, I'm half in love with you. I'd give anything for you to take a chance on us. There's never been a woman in my life I couldn't stop thinking about 24/7, someone I craved to be with all day and all night. You've become an addiction I don't want to recover from."

God, he was pushing all the right buttons. Not wanting to think anymore, just feel, she leaned in and brushed her lips against his. His eyes widened, but instead of kissing her back, he pulled away. "Be very sure, Haven. I want you to be positive you're not going to regret this, because I don't think I'll be able to walk away from you if you do. This isn't a one-night stand or just a fling until the op is over."

Her hand trailed seductively down his T-shirt-covered torso, over the waistband of the tan shorts he'd worn to bed, and further to the hard bulge underneath. His breath hitched, and he groaned as his hips flexed forward. Haven placed soft kisses over his whiskered jawline. "I won't ever regret this. It's been a long time since I've wanted someone for more than one night or a weekend—but with you, it's beyond that. I'm falling for you. I've tried to fight it, but I can't anymore—I surrender. Remind me what it's like to be alive again, Frisco. Make me scream your name."

Thrusting his hand into her hair, Frisco held her head in place as his greedy mouth took possession of hers. She parted her lips, inviting him in. He didn't hesitate, plunging his tongue inside and dueling with hers. Shifting onto his back, he took her with him until she was lying on top of him. His hands skimmed down her torso and grabbed the hem of her tank top. Dragging the fabric upward, he kissed her chin. "Can you lift yourself up a second?"

Putting her weight onto her arms, she gave him room to pull the shirt over her head. She then relaxed on top of him again, and he tossed the garment aside. Her lacy, pink bra went next. Frisco then rolled them over until Haven was on her back and he was on his side next to her. Staring at her bare chest with lust-filled eyes, he reached back and grabbed a handful of his shirt and yanked it up and off. A split second later his mouth latched onto her right breast, and he sucked on the taut peak. Haven cried out as pure pleasure shot through her. Her hands went to the back of his head to hold him there. His tongue flicked back and forth over the one nipple while his fingers found the other, teasing it. His free hand skimmed down her abdomen, and cupped her mound before pulling on the string of her cotton shorts. Haven reveled in the feel of his soft skin over the hard, powerful muscles in his back.

Frisco pushed her shorts and underwear down and found her wet and ready for him. Haven thanked her lucky stars she'd trimmed things down there in the shower yesterday as he left her breasts and licked his way down her torso. After removing the last of her clothing, he spread her legs and settled between them. He kissed her inner thigh and lifted his gaze to hers with a raised eyebrow in a silent inquiry. Haven fell for him even more at that moment. She nodded and her husky voice was filled with want and need as she said, "Yes, I felt it. Please, do it again."

He complied with her request. "Tell me if something hurts or doesn't feel right, baby. This is all about you right now. I want you to close your eyes and let me discover what you like."

Haven's heart wanted to beat out of her chest. She stared at Frisco for a few moments, but when it was clear he wasn't continuing until she shut her eyes, she followed his order. The first thing she felt was him kiss and then nibble on her other thigh. He returned to the first one and did the same, only this time a little higher . . . closer to where she wanted him the most. He cupped the back of her knees and gently pushed them toward her chest, exposing her even more.

Grabbing handfuls of the fitted sheet on either side of her, she twisted them as Frisco ran his tongue up her slit, groaning. "Damn, you taste delicious."

He did it again, this time plunging his stiffened tongue inside her, causing Haven to cry out. "Oh! Yes! Frisco!"

As he licked, nibbled, and sucked on her folds, his fingers found her clit and tormented the tiny bud. Haven squirmed as he stoked the flames starting to consume her. Her blood was like lava in her veins. His talented mouth and hands caused her body to sing in a way she'd thought it would never do again. His tongue alternated between flattening and dragging over her labia and becoming rigid, before impaling her.

Haven was drowning in a sea of pleasure, and, without warning, her climax slammed into her. She shrieked Frisco's name as she writhed and shook uncontrollably, her back arching off the bed as he wrung every ounce of ecstasy from her body. Multi-colored lights flashed behind her eyelids as she gasped for air. She wasn't a stranger to orgasms, but never before had it been more than just a sexual release. This man had taken her to heights she'd never known existed. She felt like she was floating among the clouds in the sky, as she luxuriated in a euphoric descent.

Finally, she opened her eyes and found him staring at her, a satisfied grin on his face along with the evidence of her completion. The corners of her mouth lifted upward in a lazy smile as her breathing slowed to normal. In a mellow daze, she basked in the afterglow. "Wow! That . . . was incredible."

He gave her swollen clit one last kiss. "Glad you liked it, but we're just getting started, baby. I hope you're not hungry, because I don't think we're leaving this room before lunchtime . . . or maybe, dinner." Releasing her legs, Frisco rolled off her to the edge of the bed and stood. He quickly shucked off his shorts and underwear, grabbed his wallet from the night stand, and retrieved a condom. She watched, with renewing lust, as he ripped open the foil package and removed the latex circle. Like the rest of his toned physique, his cock was a thing of beauty. It was long, thick, and erect against his lean, hard abdomen as he rolled the protection down over the dark purple crown.

Climbing back onto the bed, he crawled up her body, kissing, nipping, and licking her flesh on the way up to her mouth. She tasted herself on his lips and tongue, as her hands roamed over his shoulders and back. Looming over her, he reached down and lined up the tip of his cock with her pussy, then rocked his hips against hers. Slowly, he entered her, sheathing himself within her slick heat.

"Damn, baby. You're so tight. Please say I'm not hurting you." He clearly had scant control over his urge to fuck her with abandon but he somehow managed to hold onto it.

"I'm . . . fine. Oh, please! More, Frisco! Don't stop!"

His length and girth stretched her inner walls, as he went deeper with each restrained thrust. Leaning most of his weight on his forearms, he dropped his brow to her shoulder as he withdrew and advanced again until finally he was buried to the hilt inside her.

Lifting his head, he stared into her eyes, taking in her every response as he made love to her at a maddeningly slow pace. Haven dragged her hands down his torso and clutched his hips, digging her fingernails into his taut ass cheeks. "F-Faster, please!"

His hips picked up speed at her urging. A tornado of mixed sensations ripped through her body as his pelvic bone struck her clit with each thrust. The onslaught was too much for her to even try to hold back, and, once again, she screamed his name as she flew apart. Her walls quivered and clenched around him, making him groan and curse as his body tensed. With one final, near-violent plunge into her depths, he stiffened and roared his release.

Finally depleted, he collapsed on top of her, yet kept most of his weight on his arms as his chest heaved for oxygen. His pecs brushed against her still sensitive nipples with each ragged breath. Moments passed before he mumbled into her neck, "Does your pharmacy deliver?"

Bewildered at his question, all she could manage was, "Huh?"

"I don't want to leave this bed and I only have one more condom. We're going to need a lot more than that."

CHAPTER 15

GRABBING HIS SODA, FRISCO TOOK A SWIG, BEFORE putting it back down next to his empty plate. Slim made a damn good burger. This was the third different one Frisco had gotten over the past week and a half, and each one tasted better than the last. He was determined to sample every version on the menu before deciding which was his favorite. It would be a hard choice, but he was willing to give it a try.

It was a beautiful day, and he hadn't had trouble convincing Haven to come to the park for lunch after their side-by-side physical therapy sessions. She was getting stronger as each day went by, but was still unable to put all her weight on her legs without assistance. However, her progress, thus far, was a great motivator for her to stick with the rehabilitation. The therapists agreed it was only a matter of time before she could stand on her own. As for Frisco, he probably had another two or three weeks before he'd be cleared for full duty again. Part of him couldn't wait, but the other part wanted to stay as the Deimos-Army go-between. The mission obviously wouldn't last forever, but working with Haven every day and sleeping in her bed every night was becoming a hard-core habit he didn't want to break. He was worried that when the mission was over, she'd try to kick him out of her life again because she was too scared to see what the future might bring them. He was determined to fight for what he knew was right. He'd always heard that when you met the person you were destined to spend the rest of your life with, you'd feel it in your gut—and it was true. Now he just had to convince Haven it wasn't indigestion.

"So . . . tell me how you hooked up with Deimos." He'd told her all about his family, friends, and past, but she hadn't been as forthcoming about her own. If this was going to work between the two of them, she'd have to learn to open up to him. He hadn't said a word to her about the nightmare she'd had the other night when she'd mentioned her mother and someone named Tara. He'd discreetly asked Avery about Haven's past, but she said she was as clueless about it as he was. He wasn't sure if he believed her but he let it go. Carter had told him that neither he nor Jordyn knew about their fellow operative's past either, so Frisco was going to have to get it from the horse's mouth or not at all.

She raised an eyebrow at him as she swallowed a french fry. "I was recruited." That's all she offered him, and her hesitation prompted him to spin his hand in circles, encouraging her to continue. She sighed and rolled her eyes. "You want the whole sordid story, don't you?"

"I'd like to hear it, yes."

"Fine," she huffed. Her gaze went to the small lake behind him, and she took several moments before she spoke again. "I grew up in Battle Creek, Michigan. My father walked out on my mom, my sister, and me when I was four . . . Tara was six months at the time. As far as I know, my mother never heard from him again. She tried for years to have him tracked down for child support, but it was like he disappeared off the face of the earth. I used my contacts a few years ago to find him—intent on making him suffer and hand over all the money we'd been denied over the years. I wanted to donate it to a charity to help single mothers. Apparently, though, he'd been leading a double life—the name on my birth certificate was an alias. Turns out he was a bigamist who'd illegally married my mom, but I guess he decided he didn't want two families or couldn't handle it. The whole time Mom had been trying to track him down, he was only a hundred miles away, living with family number one. He died about two years before I found out who he really was. He'd never lost his wandering eyes and hands, and a mistress's husband shot the two of them after walking in on them one afternoon. Once I found that out, I let it drop. His legal, first wife and kids didn't need to know he had other kids out there. They were dealing with enough crap. Why should I make them suffer for his sins? Going after his meager estate would have just rubbed salt in their wounds. In fact, the guy that killed him, saved me the trouble."

Frisco remained silent. He didn't think she was kidding, but he also doubted she would've killed someone in cold blood, that wouldn't have been an authorized hit.

"Anyway, Mom did her best to raise Tara and me. We called ourselves the Three Musketeers. Things were tight growing up, but Mom always found inexpensive ways for us to have fun. She was a great woman. After my father disappeared, she got a job as a secretary at a small advertising firm. Over the years, they grew, and she got an education from the ground up. When I was old enough to watch Tara for a few hours each night, Mom went back to college and got her degree. I was twenty-one and finishing up college—pre-law—when she got a huge promotion to vice president at the same firm she'd been working for all those years. Tara and I were thrilled for her. Mom had really come into her own. She'd even been dating this nice guy for a few months. Nothing serious, as far as I knew, but he was good to her." Haven took a sip of her soda, but Frisco could tell she was lost in her memories. Her gaze was still everywhere but on him. If that made it easier for her to talk, it was fine with him.

"The promotion came in right before summer, and Mom decided she was going to start treating us to the big vacations we'd never had growing up, but had always wanted. The first one we took was to London and Dublin. For two weeks, we went everywhere we could and saw places we'd only read about or saw online. It was awesome, and Mom said we were starting a new tradition of traveling to new countries every year. The following spring break, we chose Paris and Madrid. I was going to be doing a summer internship in preparation for law school, so we went in March . . . of 2004."

Frisco's stomach sank. He had a feeling he knew where this was going, and it wasn't good—not that he'd expected it to be, based on her nightmare. But Haven continued as if she needed to get it off her chest. "Again, we had so much fun. We'd been in Madrid for three days, and I'd woken up early that last morning and convinced Mom and Tara to get up too, even though my sister wanted to sleep late." A sad smile appeared then faded quickly. "We were going to take an hour trip to San Lorenzo de El Escorial and decided to eat breakfast when we got there. A little after seven in the morning we left the hotel and walked to catch the train from the Atocha station."

Where three of ten terrorist bombs, planted by members of al Qaeda, had exploded about twenty or thirty minutes later . . . shit.

Her voice had trailed off as tears began to roll down her cheeks. Frisco stood, rounded the table, picked her up in his arms, and sat again with her on his lap. "It's okay, baby. Sh. It's okay."

A combination of a sob and hiccup escaped her as she buried her face into his neck. It took a few moments for her to regain her composure while he held her tightly in his arms, stroking her hair and back. Finally, she took a deep breath. "W-We were waiting for the train, and I had to go to the restroom. Mom and Tara were waiting on the platform for me, not that far away. I was walking out of the ladies' room . . . there was a fl-flash of light, a deafening boom, and scorching heat. I was thrown backward through the doorway."

She took a deep, ragged breath, then let it out slowly. "That's all I remember. I woke up that night and found out 192 people had been killed and over 2000 injured after bombs exploded throughout the rail system. It took me four days to get confirmation that Mom and Tara had been killed instantly. I had a bad concussion, a couple of broken ribs, and my arm was busted too. The day before I was scheduled to be released and flown back to the States by the embassy, Gene McDaniel walked into my room and made me an offer. I would be listed among the dead and go work for the United States government, fighting terrorism. It took me all of two hours before

I called the number he left and took the job. I allegedly died from complications during emergency brain surgery the next day."

A thought popped into Frisco's head, and he took advantage of her pausing to catch her breath. "How'd you get on McDaniel's radar? I mean—" He cut himself off as the answer became clear. "You were trying to get in the FBI or CIA, weren't you? That's what you were going to do with your law degree."

Haven nodded and wiped her eyes with the back of her hand. "The FBI. That's where my summer internship was going to be. When Homeland Security got the list of victims' names, the other federal agencies were interested in learning everything about them, too, especially the survivors. With my family gone, my schooling and desire to become an FBI agent, topped off with needing a way to deal with my anger and grief, Gene figured I'd fit in perfectly with Deimos—and he was right. If I hadn't been able to throw myself into my training, I honestly think I would've become self-destructive.

"The only things I have from my old life is one photo of Mom and Tara, and my grandmother's wedding ring that my mom wore all the time—Gene retrieved it for me from the morgue. Oh, and three challenge coins from when my grandfather—my mom's dad—was in the 101st Airborne in Vietnam—Gene managed to get them from our house. I was able to keep the ring and coins because my mom's relatives were never close to us, so nobody would miss them. I used to keep them in a safety deposit box that couldn't be traced to me, but now they're in my safe at the house. If anyone discovers them, it won't matter anymore if they find out I'm not who I've pretended to be all these years since I'm no longer a field operative."

Another sob was wrenched from her chest as the loss of her family and her identity hit her again. Frisco kissed her temple as more tears flowed. If anyone around them noticed her crying, they kept their distance. The usual sounds of the park and Frisco's comfort seemed to calm her. He brushed his lips across her cheek. "Why do you think their deaths are your fault?"

His words startled her, and she tilted her head as her eyes narrowed at him. "How did—"

"You were blaming yourself the other night in your sleep. You were having a nightmare and telling your mom and Tara it was your fault and you were sorry ... why?"

Wiping her wet cheeks, she said, "If we'd slept in

like Tara wanted to, we never would have been there."

"Oh, baby. Don't do that to yourself. A few months ago, Ghost told me not to live in the world of 'what if'—I'd only drive myself crazy—and he was right."

"About carrying me to the chopper?"

He nodded. "Yeah. I was afraid I'd made your injury worse, but I didn't have a choice. We had to get you and Reardon out of there.

"Everyone who's gone through something bad in their lives has those thoughts—what if I'd slept late, what if I'd gotten up early, what if I'd made a right turn instead of a left. Bad things happen to good people; it's an unfortunate fact of life. We're all going to die sooner or later, and no one should take the blame for something they couldn't have seen coming and had no control over. All we can do is grieve for our friends and loved ones we've lost, then live our lives to the fullest in their honor—to make their lives and deaths mean something. I'm sure since going to work for Deimos, you've saved countless lives, far more than you ended. Now that you're taking a new direction in your career, you'll just have to find a way to continue honoring your mom and sister. You wouldn't want them to lie in bed, crying day after day if you'd been killed instead of them. You'd want them to be happy and enjoy life, doing the things you could no longer do."

"Like your friend's dad told you."

"Mr. Riggs was a great man. If it hadn't been for his words at Digger's grave site, I'm not sure I'd be in Delta. And wouldn't that be a shame, because then I'd never have met you."

A small smile returned to her face. "And saved my life."

"Exactly." Cupping her chin, he drew her closer and brushed his lips against hers. He was thrilled when she didn't pull away, instead, lifting her arms to encircle his neck. Her mouth opened, welcoming him in, and it was an invitation he couldn't refuse if he wanted to, which he didn't. His tongue sparred with hers as his cock grew hard against her hip.

"Eew, they're kissing!"

Haven ripped her mouth from his, and they both turned to see a group of two dozen or so boys and girls, around six or seven years old, walking past their picnic table. Two women, one at the front and the other at the back of the line, had to be their teachers, taking them for a short field trip. Frisco had no idea which little boy had started them all giggling with his very loud announcement, but it didn't matter. Grinning, he glanced at Haven who was also laughing, despite her pink cheeks. "Busted."

"Yup." She gave him a quick peck on the lips. "But I know somewhere we won't be interrupted . . . and it's got a bed."

Standing with her in his arms, he set her on the seat of her chair. "How fast does that van go?"

"C'MON, TARA, HURRY YOUR ASS UP!" HALLE MCBRIDE weaved through the pedestrians on the sidewalk, who were just starting their day. She'd woken up early, when it'd still been dark outside, and hadn't been able to go back to sleep. Instead of just lying there, staring at the ceiling and listening to her sister snore, she'd woken Tara and their mother, Maryann, and convinced them to start the day early. They only had a few more days of vacation before returning to Michigan and the daily grind of school and work.

Her sister was a few feet behind Halle and their mom, trying to fix the broken zipper on her cross-body purse as she walked, not entirely watching where she was going. "I'm coming, I'm coming."

"Halle, slow down," their mom chastised. "If we miss the train, there'll be another one shortly. Tara, watch

where you're going. You're going to walk right into some-one. I swear, it's like you two are little kids again." It wasn't an insult since she was smiling and looking forward to the day trip to a place they'd only seen pictures of.

Wanting to make up for all the years when their vacations had consisted of outings to the local zoo or museums on free-admission days, or window shopping at the mall, the three women were soaking up everything they could. Paris had been fun, but having taken Spanish as her second language in high school and college, Halle was enjoying Madrid even more since she could under-stand most of what was being said around them. She'd even been able to flirt with their cute waiter last night during dinner at a little restaurant near their hotel.

With her internship starting two days after the current semester ended, she was glad the McBride women had been able to schedule their trip for spring break instead. Thankfully, Tara was now in college with Halle, so they both had fifteen days off instead of the nine days their local high school had. Next year, though, with Halle in law school, they didn't know how much time they'd have. If it was only a week, they'd probably stay in the Western Hemisphere.

As they approached the Atocha station to catch the Cercanías train to San Lorenzo de El Escorial, Halle glanced over her shoulder to make sure Tara was still with them. Still moving forward, Halle walked directly into someone coming out of the entrance to the building. "Oof!" She grasped the man's arm to steady herself. "Oh, I'm so sorry!"

The Middle Eastern man glared at her and spat something in Arabic as he shoved her away from him with more force than necessary. Halle almost tripped and ended up on her ass, but her mom reached out and grabbed her around the waist, stopping her momentum. She gaped in surprise. "What the hell? I said I was sorry."

The slender man stood about six foot two and wore loose-fitting, black pants and a white dress shirt. His hands were empty while a small knapsack hung down his back. An ugly scar from an old wound ran from his left ear to the middle of his cheek—his trim beard could only hide a small portion of it. His dark hair matched the color of his eyes—eyes that were boring into her with hate and venom. "Disgusting infidels," he growled before striding away.

"Well, screw you too!"

"Halle, hush," her mother said, pulling on her arm. "Ignore him. Let's go."

Having given up on the zipper, Tara had also seen the whole thing and chimed in. "Yeah, the last thing we need on our vacation is you getting stabbed or shot by a psychotic stranger. Don't worry, someday the asshole will get his; karma's a bitch like that."

Staring after the man, Halle knew her mom and sister were right. In this day and age, with terrorists and madmen setting off bombs or walking into places and shooting everyone just for the hell of it, one couldn't be too careful anymore. With a final, silent "fuck you," to the rude bastard, she followed her mother and sister into the station. After they got their tickets and found the track they needed, Halle glanced around. "There's a bathroom over there. I'll be right back."

"Hurry," her mom said, checking her watch. "The train will be here in eight minutes."

"Don't worry. I won't miss it." Zig-zagging through the morning crowd standing on the platform, Halle made her way to the ladies' room. The screech of brakes on a metal rail announced another train's arrival as it flew into the station and came to a stop. The doors to the cars opened, and the people on board fought to exit while others pushed their way in.

After making use of the restroom's toilet and washing her hands, Halle rubbed her hands under the hot air of a dryer on the wall. Striding to the door, she pulled on the handle and swung it open. The world detonated around her. A flash of bright light blinded her a split second before a thunderous roar filled the air, followed by *screams. The heat was unbearable as Halle was thrown off her feet and backward into a wall. Pain exploded in her head. Falling to the floor, darkness overtook her as she managed to utter one word before going still.* "Mom—"

"Haven . . . Haven, baby, wake up."

CHAPTER 16

LYING NEXT TO HAVEN IN BED, FRISCO SHOOK HER shoulder as she thrashed back and forth. It was the middle of the night, and she was having another bad dream. He was about to say her name louder when she sat straight up, her eyes opening wide, as she panted to catch her breath. Pushing himself into a sitting position, he rubbed her thigh under the covers. "Hey, you okay?"

There was a wild look in her eyes as she turned to him, still gasping for air. "I . . . I . . ."

"Sh. What is it? What were you dreaming about?"

She shook her head. Instead of answering him, she flung the covers off her body and swung her legs so they were hanging off the bed. Reaching for the wheelchair, she brought it closer and swiftly transferred from the bed to the seat. Confused, Frisco climbed out of bed and grabbed his shorts from the floor. Before he even had a chance to put them on over his boxer briefs, Haven was heading out the door.

"Hey! Haven, what's wrong?" He followed her into the office and as she began booting up the computers, he pulled on his shorts, then stood behind her with his arms across his bare chest.

"I know who he is . . . I mean, I don't know exactly who he is, but I know where I recognized him from." Her fingers flew over the keyboard.

"Who? The guy from the wedding?"

"Yeah. Talking about my mom and sister during lunch must have triggered it. Middle Eastern descent, about forty years old, dark hair and beard, and he had this—this scar on his left cheek that started at the bottom of his ear. I ran into the same man right before we entered the train station in Madrid—literally. He was an asshole and called us disgusting infidels or something like that."

Taking a deep, calming breath, Frisco placed his hands on her shoulders and squeezed gently. "Are you sure, baby? That was an awfully long time ago, and both times preceded a tragic event."

"I'm absolutely positive, Frisco. This isn't a game my mind is playing with me." She glanced over her shoulder at him. "I'm also sure he's Mr. Smith—or works for him—and was involved in both terror attacks. And now he's looking for a trifecta using the nuke this time. Wherever he plans on detonating that thing, it's somewhere in the US—I feel it in my gut."

He stared into her eyes for a moment, but her faith in her memory didn't waiver. "I'm *positive*."

"Okay," he conceded. "Let's find out who he really is."

HAVEN RAN A HAND DOWN HER FACE AS SHE REACHED for the bottle of water Frisco had placed next to her keyboard earlier. Her eyes were dry and tired from staring at her multiple computer monitors for the past eight hours. One would think a man of Middle Eastern ancestry, with a noticeable scar and probable ties to al Qaeda, would be easy to track down. *Not.* There were thousands of potential suspects from the al Qaeda *and* ISIS watch lists for her to go through, many of which had facial scars for one reason or another. And the list seemed to be growing every day as more were identified.

She and Frisco had been in contact with practically everyone by this point, and each time she had to convince them she wasn't imagining things. Kenny, Carter, and Jordyn had been easy to sway, having worked with her for years and had relied on her hunches before—and this was far more than a hunch. Currently in Washington, Gene McDaniel was also on board with her, but the president and the Army had been a little tougher to sell it to. They wanted a name and more proof this wasn't a figment of her imagination.

Frisco had been on the phone all day with the three Delta teams, who were still stationed on the Texas/Mexico border, and his colonel. Everyone was in a holding pattern waiting for the elusive Mr. Smith to contact Preston Ward. Down in San Antonio, Kenny was hard at work on his computer trying to narrow down suspects for her, as were the other analysts in California, but ultimately, it came down to Haven identifying the guy. Whoever the bastard was, she prayed he wasn't so far under the radar they didn't have anything on him. Some of these guys spent years in the United States, the United Kingdom, France, Spain, and any other country they hated for the freedoms the citizens had, hiding in plain sight. They held down normal jobs, socialized with coworkers, and barbecued with their neighbors, who they could easily kill the next day without blinking an eye.

With Roxie on her heels, Avery walked into the office and placed a turkey sandwich and potato chips on the desk in front of Frisco, who was currently talking with Ghost, getting an update. The older woman handed a second plate to Haven. "Eat. You barely touched your breakfast. You should also come out to the living room and let me help you with your stretches. You've been sitting there far too long."

"I've got too many photos to go through." Her eyes never leaving the screen in front of her for more than a split second, she picked up a chip and tossed it in her mouth. "But thanks for the lunch. I didn't realize how hungry I was." She was about to grab another one, when her phone rang. Snatching it up, she glanced at the screen before connecting the call. "Hey, Jordyn, what's—"

"He's named the meeting spot. We have two hours to get to the Paseo Reforma in Nuevo Laredo. Kenny's shooting you an email with the details, and then we're running out the door."

"What? He wants to meet in a fucking mall?" Haven heard Frisco jump to his feet behind her and tell Ghost to hang on. "But that's got to be almost a three-hour drive into Mexico from San Antonio."

"Guess he figures Preston can afford to find faster transportation. We're headed for the airport—got a chopper standing by. We'll call you when we land in Laredo and meet up with the Deltas."

Haven sighed, heavily. This was the first time she'd been this involved in a mission since her last one as a field operative, and she was being left behind. It royally sucked. "All right."

"Hey . . . don't give me that sad-sack bullshit. We need you. Get plugged into the mall's security cameras and find this bastard. You know what he looks like, we don't. It's not like the Deltas can waltz in there, wearing camos, with guns blazing. The mall was one of the targets on their list, but this is going to be a fly-by-the-seat-of-our-pants mission for all of us, and you're in the pilot's seat. Now get to work and don't make me call Frisco to kick your sorry ass."

She snorted. Leave it to Jordyn to call her out. "Yes, bi-otch! And you take care of my boy down there. Anything happens to Kenny, and I'll get out of this chair just to kill you."

"There's the kick-ass woman we all know and love. Talk to you when we land."

Operation Cliffhanger was a go. Playing with a stress ball that had been on Haven's desk, Frisco stared at the three monitors in front of him. The Deimos analysts back in California had hacked into the camera system and transferred control to the computers in Haven's office. Each screen was broken up into sections of four. Haven and Avery were on either side of him, watching their assigned feeds which were from different cameras located throughout the mall and/or the body cams hidden on the individual operatives, including Carter, Jordyn, and Reardon. The latter's was in a fake pair of glasses he was wearing.

All three Delta teams had hightailed it to the mall, in civilian clothing that hid their weapons, as soon as they had the location. Because of the border crossing, they'd only been able to smuggle in their handguns. Their assault rifles and body armor had been left in Texas, which no one was thrilled with.

Almost every contingency had been coordinated over the past two weeks, so they'd been ready for almost anything. Unfortunately, *almost* was not everything.

Ghost's team had gotten there first, while the other two had taken helicopters to a nearby airport where rented vans were waiting for them to drive into Mexico. When they arrived at the mall, everyone was broken up into teams of two or three operatives, covering as much of the interior and exterior of the building as possible. With a mall that size, though, and hundreds of shoppers, they still couldn't cover every corner of the place.

Behind Frisco, the colonel was overseeing the entire operation, having arrived shortly after being notified. However, knowing his teams could handle the mission without input from him, he let everyone do their jobs. If he was needed, he'd step in.

They had fifteen more minutes before "Mr. Smith" was supposed to approach "Preston Ward" in the crowded food court. The red-haired Reardon, dubbed "Ginger" for the mission, had on the red baseball cap, jeans, and green shirt Smith had instructed him to wear as he sat alone at a table for two, pretending to eat lunch. In reality, the guy looked like he would puke if he put anything in his stomach from the image on one of Haven's screens. She tried to calm him down. "Kenny, take deep breaths. You're going to be fine. Carter and Jordyn are twenty feet away, and you're surrounded by Deltas. Nothing's going to happen to you. Stop fidgeting and don't answer me; you'll give away the fact you're in contact with someone." It was the same thing she'd already said to him, several times, through the tiny listening device in his ear since he'd walked into the mall by himself. Jordyn and Carter had followed at a discreet distance, keeping him in sight the entire time.

In addition to his two bodyguards, there were five Delta members scattered around the food court. With their scruffy, non-military appearances, they blended in quite well with the other mall patrons. Since it was very easy for Americans with passports to cross the border, via one of three international bridges, there was a mixed crowd of Caucasians and Hispanics, so none of the operatives looked out of place. The rest of the Deltas were spread out over the entire mall, watching all the entrances and exits to both the mall itself and the area around the food court. The cameras Avery was monitoring included those in the back hallways behind the stores, where someone might question any non-employees seen back there.

Frisco's knee jiggled up and down. It was killing

him not being there to back up his teammates in person, but he still had their sixes, even if it was only through the use of cameras and microphones. "Five minutes and counting. Confirm." Each two- or three-man team came over the air, giving updates on their locations and statuses. So far, no one had seen anyone out of the ordinary. They had no idea if Smith was coming alone, with a small army, or something in between.

With three minutes left on the countdown clock, Jordyn announced, "Black shirt, black jeans, Middle Eastern, five foot ten, dark hair and beard, carrying a blue knapsack by the elevators, and wearing headphones."

Sliding her mouse across its pad, Haven moved the camera closest to the food court's elevators. Finding the target, she zoomed in and took several screen shots of the man before widening the lens view again. Somewhere in the mall, a poorly-paid security guard was probably wondering what the hell was going on with changing camera angles—if he'd even noticed and wasn't sound asleep at the moment.

As they watched, the man Jordyn had spotted stood in place and scanned the food court, before looking directly at Reardon sitting in the middle of everyone else eating lunch. Examining the screen shots, Haven shook her head and frowned. "That's not him. That's not the guy from the wedding."

"Well, he's headed toward Ginger," Jordyn responded. "Kenny, relax—everything is fine. Take a sip of your soda or something. Look to your left, away from him. Do *not* make eye contact with him unless he stops and says something to you."

There was silence over the comms while the man they now had under surveillance strode across the busy food court, but instead of stopping, he walked past Reardon and sat at an empty table, facing him. Seconds ticked by. While Carter, Jordyn, and Frisco kept their eyes on both the Deimos geek and the possible suspect, the others continued to look for other potential threats. They had no idea if the guy with the knapsack was the real Mr. Smith, a scout for him, or just some random guy looking to sit for a few minutes. Haven was scanning the crowded mall, zooming in on anyone who might be the man she was sure was behind all this.

Suddenly, there was a flash of bright light on more than half of the monitors focused on different areas around the mall, before they went dark. The sounds of multiple explosions came through loud and clear over the comm units, followed by a lot of cursing, coughing, and screams coming from the panicked occupants of the mall. Then to add to the chaos, shrill fire alarms began to blare.

Ghost barked over the commotion in the background, "Report! Cliff Two or Three!"

For a tense moment there was no response, then Carter coughed harshly into his microphone. "Cliff Three! Smoke canisters in the food court! Lost Ginger . . . repeat . . . lost Ginger!

CHAPTER 17

"REARDON, ACKNOWLEDGE IF YOU CAN HEAR ME," Carter demanded.

After three seconds without a response, Ghost asked, "Who's got eyes on the principal? Base?"

"Negative," Frisco replied. "We lost half the cameras."

He, Avery, and Haven frantically scanned through the few mall feeds they were still receiving, along with those from the body cams. The operatives were fighting their way through the throngs of people who were screaming and running for the exits. The jostling, smoke-filled images made it difficult to clearly see anything or anyone.

"How the hell did we lose only half?" the colonel asked from behind Frisco.

One of the analysts in California, listening in on the operation, came over a speaker attached to Haven's computer. "Their CCTV is running on two different frequencies. We hacked into both. Only one got knocked out."

Frisco was trying to figure out if they got lucky or screwed with the setup—not that it made a difference at this point.

"Find him, Base!" Ghost ordered. "Teams, sit-rep! Anyone hurt?" Everyone checked in and denied being incapacitated. If there were any injuries, they were minor and could be dealt with later. However, they did report there were injuries and probable deaths among the mall shoppers. At least four bombs had been detonated in various parts of the 425,174 square foot, one-floor building, while more smoke grenades had added to the panic and confusion. That was probably to disguise any escape route without cutting it off.

"Two tangos who threw the smoke grenades are down and out," Jordyn announced. "Any sign of our boy?"

Haven brought up the view from Reardon's hidden camera, which was shaking as he moved quickly in an unknown direction. Through the heavy, white smoke the occasional dark forms of people scrambling for safety could be seen. He pushed open a door and ended up in a corridor where there was far less smoke, but there was no way to tell which one he was in or what direction he was heading.

Frisco gave the intel to the team. "It looks like Ginger is in one of the hallways behind the stores. Unknown direction."

"Copy that," Ghost replied. "Teams, cover the corridors."

The operatives scrambled to find their principal. Since it hadn't taken long for Kenny to enter the hallway, it was most likely one of four nearest the food court. Each, however, ran in a different direction, with more than one exit along its length.

"Wh-Where . . . *cough* . . . are we going?"

"Oh, thank God," Haven said with relief at the sound of Reardon's voice which had not received a verbal response. However, when he stumbled forward, it was a good guess he'd been shoved from behind. Since they could only see in the direction he was looking in, it was impossible to tell how many suspects were with him and what weapons they had. "Kenny, cough *three* times fast if you can hear me."

A single cough was the only response. She tried again. "Kenny, cough three times." Again, she didn't get the correct response. "Shit. His earpiece must've come out. Damn it, Kenny, where are you?"

Shifting her gaze to a different monitor, she rapidly clicked through the feeds that were still working. Suddenly, she stopped and went back to one that was from a camera in the parking lot. Hundreds of people were streaming out of the mall, running for their lives, but something else had caught Haven's attention. Making the quarter-sized, streaming image fill the full screen, she focused on a white van parked in an alleyway, backed up to a loading dock. Frisco kept one eye on the view from Reardon's hidden camera, and the other on what Haven was doing. She zoomed the camera in on the windshield. Two people were in the front seat, and she focused on the driver first. "Middle Eastern, but not my guy. Ten to one this is where they're headed, though."

Frisco agreed since the men seemed unaffected by the bedlam occurring throughout the mall and parking lot. He quickly referenced the building's floor plan he'd printed out earlier. "That's what? Loading Dock C?"

She checked the lettering at the top right corner of the feed. "Yeah, Dock C." She had the other man in the center of her screen, but he was turned in the seat, watching the doors leading in the mall. "Come on, passenger, look at the pretty birdie."

Not waiting to see if it was the guy she was looking for, Frisco forwarded the info to his teammates. "Operation Cliffhanger. Corridor 8, heading for Loading Dock C. Repeat. Corridor 8, Loading Dock C. White, commercial van. Two possible tangos in the front seat. Unknown if anyone is in the back."

Ghost and several other Deltas confirmed they copied the transmission. The mission leader rattled off assignments designed to block in the suspects before they could escape with their hostage.

"That's him! Frisco, look! That's him!" Haven was pointing at the passenger who had a scar on his left cheek. "He's a lot thinner than I remember, but it's definitely him."

"I'll be damned," he muttered before speaking into his microphone. "Operation Cliffhanger, proceed with caution. Tango in passenger seat confirmed. Repeat. Tango confirmed."

Haven widened the view of the camera lens just as the double doors to the mall flew open. A terrified-looking Reardon was shoved forward by a third suspect, the guy with the knapsack from the food court. Frisco alerted the team as the scarred terrorist climbed out of the passenger seat and approached his comrade and their captive, a little slower than expected. "Ginger on Loading Dock C with third tango. Don't lose him, boys!"

He hadn't needed to issue the directive, knowing his team wouldn't let him down. Before the suspects had any idea what was happening, two dark SUVs raced in from opposite directions and skidded to a stop at the far end of the loading dock's alleyway, blocking the van's escape route. Trigger, Lefty, Oz, and Grover climbed out and aimed their weapons at the suspects' vehicle. Blade, Beatle, and Truck, came running out from a main, public exit, and used the corner of the building at the entrance to the alleyway as cover. Carter, Jordyn, and another Delta did the same on the opposite side. Meanwhile, Ghost, Fletch, Coach, and Hollywood moved into position, just inside the double doors of the mall, preventing anyone from reentering. Up on the roof, several more operatives aimed their guns at the tangos below them. All avenues of escape had been effectively cut off in a matter of seconds.

Beside Haven, Frisco could practically feel the fear rolling off of her as she stared at her unarmed friend. The moment Scarface realized he was trapped, he grabbed Reardon around the neck and put the muzzle of his 9mm pistol to his head. He stood with his back against the outer brick wall of the building and began to shout in Arabic. The gist of it was he demanded they let him and his buddies go or he was going to kill his hostage. Frisco reached over and grasped Haven's shaking hand in silent support. While he had the same sense of helplessness she had to be feeling, both of them had to trust their teams would bring the standoff to a swift end, with only the tangos ending up in body bags.

They were at a Mexican standoff—pun intended. The good guys just had to find a way to change the status quo in their favor. Scarface was still yelling his demands, but even he had to know this wasn't going to end well for him and the other two suspects.

Suddenly, there was a burst of automatic gunfire as the driver aimed his weapon through the open window toward one of the SUVs blocking his escape. The attack was immediately countered by the operatives who had clear shots. The tango was riddled with bullets and when he was no longer a threat, the guns went silent again.

On the opposite side of the van, Scarface was still holding his hostage in front of him, banking on the fact his enemies wouldn't shoot the redhead, as Ghost spoke in Arabic, trying to get him to surrender. Most of the Deltas knew enough of the language to communicate if a translator wasn't available. Meanwhile, the third suspect had realized he was a prime target, with nothing or no one to hide behind, and dropped to the ground, covering his head as if that would keep him from being killed.

From around the corner of the building, Carter spoke softly, "Someone give me the tango's height, how far away he's standing from the wall, and if I have a clear shot."

Frisco's eyebrows went up as he realized what the spy was planning on doing, even though he knew it was necessary. If they didn't act fast, the cops would be there soon, adding to the chaos, and it would be impossible for them to differentiate between the good guys and bad guys.

Oz was in the best position to relay the information as he stood behind the open driver's door of one of the SUVs. "Six foot one, not slouching, two-three inches max from the wall. Clean shot if you wait for my signal. Ghost, count to three and give him a distraction."

The six-foot-four-inch Deimos spy stepped away from the brick wall he'd been leaning against and then turned to face it. Bringing his weapon up so it was seventy-three inches above the ground, he patiently waited. About twenty feet into the alleyway Scarface was pissed and getting desperate. When Ghost insulted him by saying "Lick my ass, you shit," in Arabic, the suspect swung his weapon away from Reardon's head and aimed it toward the double doors his tormentor was hiding behind.

Immediately, Oz gave the go order. "Now!"

As Avery, Haven, Frisco, and the colonel held their breaths, staring at the screen, Carter took a wide step to the right into the mouth of the alley. As soon as the muzzle of his gun cleared the corner of the building, he fired. Scarface's head snapped to the left as he was shot about an inch behind his right temple. A burst of blood, bone, and brains splattered everywhere as the bullet exited the other side of his skull. Reardon let out an involuntary scream, as the dead man's arm fell away from his throat.

The operatives swarmed into the alleyway, as Ghost barked orders. Oz grabbed Reardon, who was frozen in shock, the left side of his face covered in Scarface's blood, and practically threw him into the nearest SUV. Trigger, and Lefty jumped in, too, and within seconds they were hauling ass away from the scene. After confiscating his 9mm and frisking him for other weapons, Carter and Jordyn did the same thing with the third suspect, who was still lying face down on the ground, begging for his life. With Truck at the wheel, the American spies disappeared with their captive who would be interrogated as soon as they got him to a secure location. Back in California, where he'd been listening in and watching the live feeds, Gene McDaniel ordered his computer geeks to erase the last ten minutes of the recordings from the mall's security cameras.

Through the comm units, Frisco heard the sirens announcing the approaching first responders. The pandemonium in the crowded parking lot, where people were still running for safety and trying to figure out what had happened, would, hopefully, give the operatives a few more minutes before the cops reached the loading dock. Some people undoubtedly heard the gunshots and would point them in the direction they came from. If the team was lucky, no one had been aware of what had been happening in the alleyway or close enough to use their cell phones to record a video during those few minutes. While Beatle took photographs of the two dead men, Blade worked quickly to scan their finger-prints into a small, portable device Jordyn had given him, as Haven explained to him over the comm unit how it worked.

Ghost and Fletch checked the interior of the van

for the bomb, even though it was doubtful the suspects had brought it with them. Ghost confirmed that theory moments later. "No suitcase. Repeat. No suitcase. But there are a few more pipe bombs."

"Copy that," Frisco responded, before glancing over his shoulder at the colonel.

The older man muttered a curse, then said, "Have them sterilize the van for anything to do with the nuke, but leave the explosives for the Mexican authorities. Then start helping with the injured. It's a good thing my men decided to have lunch in Nuevo Laredo after a training session over the border, and interrupted the bombers' escape plan."

Frisco passed on the orders and cover story to Ghost, as the colonel stepped over to where a secure phone sat atop the wooden desk on the other side of the room. The president and director of Homeland Security were waiting for an update from him.

Pushing her chair back, Avery stood as if the past few stressful hours happened every day. "While you all finish up in here, let me go check on my roast beef." She glanced across the room, then back at Frisco, who was surprised to see a blush stain her cheeks. She cleared her throat and then said in a low voice, "Um . . . if the colonel wants to . . . um . . . stay for dinner, there's plenty."

The corners of his mouth ticked upward as he nodded once. "I'll let him know."

As she hurried out of the room with Roxie on her heels, he turned his chair just enough to see his superior. His grin grew wider when the divorced, older man subtly checked out Avery's shapely ass before she disappeared into the hallway. "I'll be damned," Frisco muttered.

"What?" Haven's voice had him spinning his chair back around to look at her. Tapping away on her keyboard, she gave him a quick glance and repeated her question. "What?"

"Nothing," he responded, shaking his head. "I'll tell you later. In the meantime, let's find that nuke so I can take you out on a real date that doesn't involve shop talk. Deal?"

She smiled for the first time since she'd awakened from her nightmare. "Deal."

CHAPTER 18

THREE DAYS LATER, JORDYN, CARTER, AND KENNY relaxed on Haven's patio as she made sure everything they needed was on the outdoor dining table. Satisfied she hadn't forgotten anything, she eyed Frisco tending the barbecue. "Do you need any help?"

Smiling, he brushed sauce over several racks of baby back ribs. "Got it covered, babe, but thanks for the offer. I'd love another beer, though, if you don't mind."

She grabbed one from the nearby cooler and rolled over to him. Her reward was a brief kiss on the lips that held the promise of something more later when they were alone.

It was a quiet celebration of a mission gone well. It hadn't taken long for the surviving terrorist-wanna-be, Sadi al-Bina, to start spilling his guts after being threatened with castration. Apparently, he was more interested in meeting the seventy-two vestal virgins than Allah himself in the afterlife. The suitcase nuke was right where he'd told them it would be, in an inconspicuous hotel room in Nuevo Laredo. The plan had been to kidnap "Preston Ward" and get the software protection dongle for free, then transport the bomb over the border and plant it in downtown Austin. Of course, they hadn't counted on the operatives of Delta and Deimos messing up that plan.

After confirming they could move the nuke without the chance of blowing it up, several Deltas had loaded it into an unmarked van, then quietly drove it to an isolated area, north of the city. They were met by members of a government-classified team, who'd flown over the border in a non-military helicopter to retrieve the device and transport it to the Waste Isolation Pilot Plant in New Mexico for disposal.

As far as the Mexican authorities knew, they'd been lucky that a few US soldiers happened to be at the mall after taking a break from training. After identifying the bombing suspects and trying to capture them, they'd been involved in a shootout, during which both terrorists were killed. Eighteen victims had died in the mall, and over seventy had been injured. Had the Americans not interfered, those numbers could have been much higher if the remaining pipe bombs had been detonated. The Mexican government was so grateful they'd willingly overlooked the fact the soldiers had somehow managed to bring their sidearms into the country without being detected.

The man Haven had recognized from both the wedding and from the terrorist attack in Madrid had been identified as Hamad el-Salik. The analysts at Deimos were still trying to track down how the man had remained off everyone's radar all these years, but one thing they'd learned was he'd planned on becoming a martyr by blowing himself up with half of the population of Austin. He'd been diagnosed with terminal brain cancer and wanted to go out with a bang—literally. With that new knowledge, Haven was even more satisfied with his violent death than she'd been several days ago and hoped he'd gone straight to Hell.

It had taken her a few hours for the reality of the day to hit her, but when it did, Frisco had been there to hold her as, once again, she'd grieved for her mom and sister. She'd sat on his lap and bawled for what felt like hours, as he held her tightly and murmured words of comfort. After that, he'd taken her to bed and made sweet love to her. Even though the mission was over, he'd slept with her each night since. Last night, he'd even taken her out on that date he'd wanted. At first, it'd been odd, sitting in a movie theater with a guy, for no other reason than to enjoy the show, but after they'd started making out in the back row, it'd felt so right. Somehow, Frisco had gotten past all her defenses, and she'd fallen in love with him. Where they were going from here, she had no idea, but wherever they went, she had a feeling it would be together, hand in hand.

Rejoining the others, Haven looked at Kenny who seemed to have completely recovered from his near kidnapping. "So, when are you going back to California? Tomorrow?"

"Nope," he answered with a smile. Haven's eyes narrowed as he continued. "I talked to Mr. McDaniel and asked if I could transfer here to work with you. He said yes."

"What? Seriously?" She was shocked but thrilled.

"Yeah. I mean, how else am I going to find the right girl someday without one of my two best wingmen . . . or wingwomen, I guess I should say."

"Look out, Texas chicks," Carter said with a teasing laugh, "there's a new geek in town."

Haven leaned over and gave her redheaded friend a peck on the cheek, which caused him to blush. "This is great. I'm going to love working with you."

"Dinner's ready," Frisco announced, placing a plate laden with ribs on the table, before going back to the barbecue to grab some baked potatoes and ears of corn.

The others moved from the sitting area around the fire pit to the table as Roxie hurried over to join them from where she'd been sleeping in the shade of a tree in the backyard. Realizing she wasn't getting any human food, she laid down next to Haven's wheelchair.

"By the way, where's Avery?" Jordyn asked as Carter filled a plate for her.

Haven's eyes sparkled as she smiled. "On a date . . . with Frisco's colonel."

"Ooooh. Good for them."

Frisco took the seat next to Haven, and before anyone could dig into their meal, he held up his beer. "A toast. To a successful mission, good friends, good times, and new beginnings. Cheers."

Everyone clinked their bottles and glasses together. "Cheers!"

LATER THAT NIGHT, AFTER THEIR GUESTS HAD LEFT, Frisco sat on the couch, moaning in pleasure. While watching a movie, now forgotten, Haven had rolled onto her stomach, unzipped his jeans, pulled his boxer briefs down, and withdrew his cock, which had responded in her hands. Taking him into her mouth, she wrapped her lips around his girth and sucked, as his hand plunged into her thick hair and palmed the back of her head. Her tongue swirled around the hard flesh from the notched tip to its base. When she tried to gain access to his balls, Frisco lifted his hips just enough to push his jeans and boxers to his knees, then relaxed again to enjoy her ministrations. She rolled his heavy sac in her hand, while her head bobbed up and down. Drops of salty and tangy pre-cum oozed from his slit and the taste urged her on.

Frisco's hand skimmed down her back, ducked under the waistband of her sweatpants, and squeezed her ass cheek. When she brought him to the back of her mouth and swallowed, he groaned, "God, baby, don't stop. That feels so good. Please, don't stop."

She loved how desperate he sounded, as if she was the only woman on Earth who could drive him to the brink of sensual insanity. Each time they made love, she regained more confidence in herself. The old Haven Caldwell was gone forever, but she liked this new one much better, even if she hadn't in the beginning. If it hadn't been for Frisco, she might never have realized she had so much to live for. Her life hadn't gone as her teenaged self had hoped it would before being irrevocably changed for the first time in Madrid and then again in Mumbai. But somehow, those traumatic events had led her to the man she was certain had been made for her. There were very few men who could truly understand what she'd been through, and even fewer she could discuss her past, fears, and career with. But Frisco got her in more ways than she'd ever expected someone could. He hadn't run away when things got tough, instead, he'd regrouped and come on even stronger. After asking a few questions about her memory of the terror suspect, he hadn't scoffed at or placated her, he'd trusted her enough to stand beside her and helped prove she'd been right.

The hand in her hair tightened, sending a tingling through her scalp that bordered on pain, but excited her even more. Frisco pulled her off his erection. "Baby, if you keep that up, I won't be responsible for drowning you. Can you straddle me?"

Giving the tip of his cock a final swipe of her tongue, she said, "I think so. If you help me."

As he retrieved one of the now ever present condoms from his wallet and quickly donned it, Haven shed her clothing, tossing them in a heap on the floor. Frisco added his T-shirt to the growing pile and kicked his jeans and boxers off. He then grabbed Haven under her arms and pulled her on top of him. She grasped the back of the couch for support as they worked together to arrange her legs on either side of his thighs. He glanced up at her. "Okay?"

"Mmm-hmm. But it'll be more than okay after you're inside me."

"Impatient, are you? Well, so am I, baby."

Using the back of the couch, Haven raised her body up, and Frisco positioned his cock at the entrance to her pussy. As she lowered herself down on top of him, he clutched her hips to give her extra support. They both moaned as he impaled her. Slowly, her body yielded to its mate's invasion until he was buried to the hilt. With his eyelids closed, Frisco held her in place for a moment, clearly trying to get himself under control and not cum too soon.

Finally, his eyes opened again, and Haven almost gasped at the love she saw in them. Her heart pounded in her chest as she realized he wouldn't say the words until he thought she was ready to hear them. It was at that moment she knew she'd fallen for him completely. There were no more doubts, no regrets, and no defenses needed. This man was the other part of her she'd never known was missing.

Leaning down, she brushed her lips against his. "One month."

His eyes narrowed. "Huh?"

"If you're still looking at me like that one month from today, I want you to move in with me. You're here every night anyway, so what's the point of having two places. Unless, that's the way you want to keep it."

His hand went to the back of her neck and

pulled her down for a hard, demanding kiss. When he released her, he flexed his hips upward. "I'm ready to move in tomorrow, baby, but if you want a month, then that's what you'll get. But don't think I'm not going to try and make it sooner—after all, I am a guy."

She smiled. "And I'm the woman who's madly in love with you."

"Well, damn. I thought it was going to take a lot longer for you to be convinced. I must be more irresistible than I thought. And just for the record, I love you too, baby."

He leaned forward, and his mouth latched onto one of her bare breasts. As he tortured the stiff peak with his lips, tongue, and teeth, he clutched her hips and set a steady pace that soon had her spiraling into space. They worked as one, raising and lowering her hips, as he thrust upward from underneath her. While perspiration coated their bodies, their breathing and heart rates increased.

"Finger your clit, baby," Frisco ordered as he moved to her other nipple to give it the same attention.

Leaving one hand clutching the back of the couch, she slid the other down between their bodies. She was smooth down there again, having gone for a waxing and a few other beauty treatments with Avery two days ago. Gene McDaniel had treated them to a day at the spa for all Haven's hard work on the case and Avery's hard work with her patient. Haven was still super sensitive down there but that made tonight even more erotic. She rubbed the tiny bud while Frisco picked up the pace. His fingers dug into her ass as he fucked her, driving her higher with every thrust of his pelvis.

Haven was on the edge, and she begged for relief. "Please, Frisco . . . oh, God, please!"

He slid down a little further on the couch, and it changed the angle of his hips. His cock stimulated her G-spot, and that was all she needed. Screaming his name, she fell into a vortex of pleasure. Her eyes slammed shut as wave after wave tumbled over her. Her orgasm triggered his, and he came inside her with a roar. Haven gasped for air as her walls quivered around his cock.

They collapsed into a mass of heated flesh and sagging limbs. Haven rested her forehead against his. She had no idea how long they stayed like that, but she startled when Frisco slid from her body, scooted to the edge of the cushion, and stood, wrapping her legs around his waist.

"Where are we going?" she asked, content to be in his arms.

"The shower. I plan on making love to you in every room of this house over the next few days, and then start all over again. Sound like a plan?"

She licked his ear. "Sounds like a great plan."

EPILOGUE

Taking a swig of his beer, Frisco sat in a chair across the unlit fire pit from Reardon, after handing over the grilling duties to Oz and Grover. There were about forty adults and a dozen or so kids spread out across the patio, backyard, and pool area at Haven's house. It was a welcome home party for both Frisco's and Ghost's Delta teams after being overseas for the past three months on a joint mission. Despite some bumps, bruises, and an isolated wound or two requiring stitches, everyone had come home safe and sound three days ago. They'd shipped out two weeks after the mission in Mexico, and Frisco had been able to join them, having been medically cleared the day before. For the first time in his career, he'd regretted having to leave a girlfriend behind, not knowing when he'd be back. But thankfully, there'd been numerous opportunities for Frisco to call or video chat, via a secure link, with Haven while they were apart. Although he would've preferred to be in her bed every night, it had given them a chance to get to know each other better. It had cemented in his mind that taking their relationship to the next level was the right thing to do. An engagement ring was practically burning a hole in the pocket of his shorts, and he was working up the courage to take a knee in front of her.

After spending a little more than twenty-four hours in bed making love to her, interspersed with breaks for food and other necessities, he'd used a debriefing meeting as an excuse to go pick out the ring. Avery had agreed to meet him at the jeweler's. The older woman had been delighted to help and was the only one at the party who knew the proposal was coming today. Out in California, his parents and sisters also knew and couldn't wait to meet his intended bride after he'd been telling them all about her whenever he'd called them. Frisco was just waiting for the right moment to ask Haven to marry him. He wanted them engaged when his team helped him move from his apartment to her house in a few days, since they'd all shipped out prior to being able to do it for the date Haven had set.

Roxie was having a grand time following the toddlers and older kids around, snatching up any food they dropped onto the ground, and getting petted by everyone. In addition to Avery, Reardon, and the Delta teams and their families, also present were Carter, Jordyn, and a few Trident operatives. Surprisingly, Ian Sawyer and his pregnant wife Angie, Brody "Egghead" Evans and his new wife, Fancy, Kip "Skipper" Morrison, and Tempest "Babs" Van Buren had flown into town yesterday at the last-minute invitation. They'd been en route to Florida from California where they'd been visiting their friend, country singer Summer Hayes, who'd been in a recent rollover car accident. Angie and Fancy had gone along to check on her, while the Trident team members were planning the security for Summer's release from the rehab hospital she was in for her injuries. She'd be returning to her new home outside of Tampa for the rest of her recovery. Babs had flown the Trident jet in place of the regular pilot who was laid up with a stomach bug. The others from the private security company hadn't been able to attend due to various assignments or busy personal lives back in Florida.

When they'd arrived, Sawyer had handed over a case of expensive scotch to Ghost who'd been confused at first. He then laughed when the Trident boss pointed to Hollywood and said, "Everyone can have some except that rat-bastard who should know better than to try and pull one over on me."

Haven had been thrilled to meet Babs and Skipper to thank them for their part in her rescue. Apparently, she'd only met a few members of the two Trident teams prior to the mission. She was currently talking to Fancy and Brody, the latter was joking about telling someone named "Mistress Roxy" there was another auburn-haired Roxie running around. He pointed at the pup who was taking a break in the shade at the moment. His wife laughed and dared him to do it. From what Frisco could overhear, after a moment's thought, the guy declined, saying he wasn't into getting whipped by a Domme.

Rolling over, with Fletch and Emily's daughter, Annie, on her lap, Haven stopped next to Frisco and leaned over for a swift kiss. The seven-year-old girl had apparently become enraptured with the Deimos operative, and vice versa, as Haven had gotten to know the girlfriends and wives of the other Deltas over the past few months. He'd been grateful they'd welcomed her with open arms. For the first time in far too many years, Haven had a group of women who were simply her friends, not coworkers, targets, or passing acquaintances.

"Look what Haven gave me, Frisco!" Beaming, Annie held out her hand. In it was a small, clear, display box holding one of the Vietnam-era, 101st Airborne challenge coins that had belonged to Haven's grandfather. The little tomboy was fascinated with anything to do with the military, especially the Army. Haven had told Frisco one night, during a video call, she knew her sister and mother would've loved little Annie and her enthusiasm. They also would've agreed with giving her one of Joseph McBride's coins, knowing she would cherish it.

"That's great, sprite. You take good care of that."

"I will." She eyed Carter as he took the chair between Frisco and Jordyn, who'd also just sat down. When the spy smiled at her scrutiny, she held up the box. "Look what Haven gave me—"

She paused and wrinkled her nose. "I'm sorry, but I forgot your name." Intelligent and wise beyond her years, the little girl had a tendency to sound like someone in their twenties or thirties, much to her parents' chagrin at times.

"It's Carter, sweetheart, and that's a really nice present. You must be a very special person for Haven to give that to you."

"I am. We're best friends." Her matter-of-fact tone almost dared anyone to disagree with her.

"Can never have too many of those," he replied with a brotherly wink at Haven.

"What's your other name? You can't have just one name."

Most of the Delta and Trident operatives within hearing distance, and a few others who were acquainted with the spy, zeroed in on the conversation. With a huge grin on her face, Jordyn rubbed Carter's shoulder with the palm of her hand. "Yes, dear. Why don't you tell Annie your full name? I'm sure she'd love to hear it. I know I would."

He growled at her under his breath, before turning back to the little girl. "My full name is T. Carter, but everyone just calls me Carter."

Annie seemed to consider that for a moment, but being her true, inquisitive self, she wouldn't drop it. "You're named after tea . . . like sweet iced tea? That's weird."

Ignoring the few chuckles around him, he shook his head. "No, not like iced tea. Just the letter T."

"That's even weirder. A few kids in school are

called by two initials, like C.J. and P.K. but they told me what the letters stand for. What does T stand for?"

Several people moved closer, including Fletch who was holding back his laughter. Haven stared at her colleague over Annie's shoulder. "Yeah, Carter, what does the T stand for? I think after all this time working with you, I should be allowed to know what your full name is."

The man glared at her before softening his gaze for the little girl again, clearly knowing she'd backed him into a corner. Apparently, it wasn't often he couldn't charm the hell out of a member of the opposite sex, no matter their age. "If I give you five dollars, will you forget it and just call me Carter?"

Tilting her head to the side, Annie thought for a moment before saying, "Make it ten dollars—I'm saving for a tank."

Laughter burst out around them as Carter pulled out his wallet with a sigh. "Fletch, you do realize you and your pretty wife are raising an extortionist, right?"

"Yup," the little girl's father said with a grin. It wasn't the first time the little imp had conned one of Fletch's associates to add to her piggy bank. "Normally, I would've cut her off at the pass, but this is too funny. Besides, your first name is one of the great mysteries in life I'd love to solve. Even Tex hasn't been able to find it." Tex was a buddy of Ghost, Fletch, and the others on their team, with a talent for uncovering intel on practically anyone. If he couldn't find it, there was a good chance no one could.

"That's because it's been completely eradicated from every computer and written record out there. The only two people who know are my boss, who recruited me and knows I'll slit his throat if he ever tells anyone, and my beautiful woman here, who will never be able to sit down again if she repeats it." He handed Annie a twenty-dollar bill. "The extra is so you can get that tank sooner and drive your daddy crazy."

Shrugging, she examined the money. "I already drive him crazy."

"Isn't that the truth," her father agreed, before tugging on a lock of her hair. "But I wouldn't want it any other way."

As Carter fended off the others trying to guess his name with some hilarious suggestions, the little girl hopped off Haven's lap and ran to find her mother to hold onto the cash for her. Haven's gaze followed her for a moment before returning to

Frisco. Rolling closer, she lowered her voice so only he could hear. "She's adorable. It's been years since I've thought about having kids, but being around her and the others lately has me thinking that one day I'd like to have some. After Mom and Tara were killed, I never thought I'd be happy again—part of a family—you've helped me prove that theory wrong. Thank you."

Frisco's heart began to beat faster. He'd never come right out and told her he wanted to marry her one day. But he'd dropped semi-obvious hints here and there, saying things like, "This is something to tell our grandkids someday" or "When we're old and gray . . ." However, this was the first time Haven had commented on something about their future together. It was as if their stars were aligning themselves and giving him a sign. *This is it. This is the time to tell her and everyone else here I plan on making her my wife.*

Getting to his feet, he reached into the side pocket of his cargo shorts and pulled out the small jeweler's box, cupping it in his hand so she couldn't see it until he opened it. Going down on one knee, he barely heard the gasps and squeals around him. He didn't even acknowledge when, from somewhere behind him, Sawyer groaned and said, "Oh, jeez, Taint-waffle. Seriously? Make it quick, will ya?"

Tuning everyone out, especially Sawyer, Frisco focused all his attention on Haven. A flash of confusion had crossed her face before turning into stunned disbelief. Her mouth dropped open, and her eyes went wide. Butterflies had taken flight in his stomach, but Frisco knew he would never be satisfied until his ring was on her finger. She was who his heart had been searching for all his life—the other half of his soul.

HAVEN'S MOUTH WENT DRY AS SHE STARED AT FRISCO down on one knee. This had to be a dream—a wonderful, crazy dream. Never since her mom and sister had been killed had she thought she'd have a normal life again. But this handsome, amazing man in front of her had made her realize she could be happy once more—she could open up her heart and love someone and have them love her back. She still had her career, but at night, that wouldn't keep her safe and warm. And there would come a day, hopefully, when she was old and gray, she could leave all that behind her and just enjoy being with Frisco for the rest of their lives.

"Haven, I know this is sudden, but to me, it feels like I've known you all my life. When I think back to the day I first laid eyes on you, before I knew how perfect you were for me, it still freaks me out. I could've lost you before I ever had the chance to fall in love with you. But I did. I fell hard, baby—face first—and I'd gladly do it again." She giggled as happy tears began to roll down her cheeks. "You're the other half of my heart and my soul—the better half. Please, make me the happiest man alive —marry me?"

A hushed silence had fallen over the party, interrupted only by a few of the smaller kids laughing and asking what was going on. Haven was still in shock—and here she'd thought *she'd* be the one surprising *him*. "On one condition."

Puzzled, his eyes narrowed as she rotated the wheels of her chair back a few inches, then locked them in place. Never taking her eyes off him, she leaned down and lifted the calf and foot rests out of the way. Placing her feet on the ground, she gripped the arms of the chair and pushed upward. It had been difficult, but she'd managed to keep it a secret for the past few days. She'd wanted everyone who'd helped her that fateful day, and every day since, to be present to see what she'd accomplished after all these months. Frisco had known she'd gained more strength in her legs while he was away on the mission, but this was going to be the first time he saw her stand without any assistance. She'd worked her ass off while he was gone. She still wasn't one hundred percent yet, and might never be, but it didn't matter. Frisco loved her regardless, and she loved him.

His eyes widened as she used all her might to stand. He jumped to his feet when she swayed forward before catching his arm. Steadying herself, she grinned as she let go again and stood without assistance. "I'll marry you as long as I get to walk down the aisle—just make it a short one." She smirked. "Think you can handle that?"

Wrapping his arms around her waist, he picked her off the ground and spun around in circles. Cheers filled the air as his lips found her ear. "I can definitely handle that. You've got yourself a deal."

I hope you enjoyed Frisco and Haven's story. I had so much fun borrowing Susan Stoker's Delta Force operatives and their families for this book and combining them with those from my Trident

Security series along with a few new characters. I look forward to writing more stories about the other covert spies at Deimos.

I'd appreciate if you took a moment to leave a review for *Handling Haven*.

IF YOU'D LIKE TO READ MORE ABOUT THE TRIDENT Security team, start with **Leather & Lace**, available on Amazon.

"NO ONE DOES ALPHA HEROES LIKE SAMANTHA A. Cole!"—**New York Times, USA Today, #1 Amazon Bestseller, and Wall Street Journal Bestselling Author, Susan Stoker**

KRISTEN ANDERS IS STARTING HER LIFE OVER AGAIN after divorcing her cheating husband. An author of several "vanilla" romance novels, she spiced up her latest one involving BDSM and it became a bestseller. Now she's researching the subject for her follow-up book and manages to get a tour of the elite, private sex club, The Covenant, and runs into the one person she never expected to see there.

Devon "Devil Dog" Sawyer is intrigued by a cute brunette he meets at a friend's Irish pub and does something he hasn't done in over twelve years. He asks her out on a date. While it might seem strange to most, Devon's only relationships since he was twenty-four have started and ended in the same place–a BDSM club.

What was supposed to be a single weekend of mutual pleasure and dirty sex, turns into something more. But while they fight their growing connection, a killer has Devon in his sights and Kristen may end up as collateral damage. Will they survive with their lives and hearts intact?

IF YOU HAVEN'T READ SUSAN STOKER'S DELTA FORCE series yet, get Book 1, *Rescuing Rayne*, here!

AS A FLIGHT ATTENDANT, RAYNE JACKSON IS USED TO cancellations, but she never dreamed her latest would lead to a whirlwind tour of London with a handsome stranger . . . or a life-altering night in his bed. One evening is all the enigmatic man can give her, and Rayne greedily takes it, despite suspecting it will never be enough.

Heading home after another extreme mission, Keane "Ghost" Bryson hadn't planned to seduce someone during his layover, but Rayne is too sweet to resist. Being a Delta Force member means lying to protect his identity, which is unfortunate, considering Rayne seems made for Ghost, right down to the tattoo on her back. For the first time in his life, regret fills him as he slips away the following morning.

Both are shocked when, months later, they meet again—under the worst possible circumstances. Seems fate has given them a second chance . . . if they can survive the terrorist situation they're in. If Rayne can forgive Ghost his lies. And if Ghost can trust Rayne to be strong enough to endure the secrets and uncertainty that come with loving a Delta Force soldier.

THE FIRST BOOK IN MY MALONE BROTHERS SERIES, *Take the Money and Run*, is also on Amazon!

WITH A GUN AND A DUFFEL BAG FULL OF CASH, Moriah Jensen is on the run from the police and ruthless drug dealers. She'd fled Chicago after her family was murdered and has spent the past four months trying to stay alive. Using an alias, she has bounced around from town to town, state to state, trying to stay at least a few steps ahead of the people chasing her.

KC Malone is on a two-week leave from his Navy SEAL team when he arrives at his uncle's beach house to find a beautiful woman pointing a gun at his chest. What the hell had he just walked in on?

When the two become reluctant, temporary housemates, KC offers to train Moriah to defend herself against an alleged abusive ex-boyfriend. But then her past catches up with her and Moriah has to decide between her love for KC and running for safety. To stay would risk both their lives. To run would mean leaving her heart behind.

MY STANDALONE NOVEL, *THE ROAD TO SOLACE* (formerly *The Friar*), won a silver medal out of over 1000 entries in the contemporary romance genre in the 2017 Readers' Favorite Awards! Get it on Amazon!

ADAM WESTFIELD IS AN EX-FRIAR JUST RELEASED from prison. Unsure of his destiny, he roams America, hoping to find a purpose . . . and forgiveness.

A widowed mother of two, Sage Hammond is struggling to keep her horse ranch afloat. Unable to find a ranch hand willing to work for meager wages, she's close to giving up. Then, an answer to her prayers appears—a quiet, handsome stranger.

Adam is falling in love for the first time in his life, however, strange things begin to happen at the ranch—things that are putting Sage and her children in danger—and he finds he's willing to sell his soul to protect them. But will it be enough?

A man trying to overcome his past. A woman trying to secure her children's future. Can they both learn to live in the present and discover that second chances do exist?

OTHER BOOKS BY SAMANTHA A. COLE

The Ultimate Price: Book 3—Coming Soon

The Hazard Falls Series

<u>*Don't Fight It: Book 1*</u>

The Blackhawk Security Series

Tuff Enough: Book 1—Coming December 2018

Stand Alone Novels

<u>*The Road to Solace*</u>

Special Projects

<u>*The Trident Security Coloring Book*</u>

<u>*Word Search For Warriors: Authors For a Cause*</u>

ACKNOWLEDGMENTS

To Susan Stoker—Thanks so much for writing kick-ass characters! You're an inspiration to many authors following in your footsteps. It was an honor to borrow Ghost, Fletch, Hollywood, and all the others. Keep your stories coming!

To Jon Guidry—Thanks for helping with 1990s computer technology and figuring out that the doohickey I was looking for was a software protection dongle!

To Marisa-rose Robyn—Thank you for the use of Roxie. I hadn't planned on having a dog in the story, but she was a beautiful addition. I hope I did her justice. Until you meet again at the Rainbow Bridge . . . woof

To my editor, Eve—I owe you so much credit for helping to make my books the best they can be for my readers. Love you!

To Judi—Thanks for another awesome cover and the inspiration to make the story better!

To my PAs, Maria, Connie, and Kelly, and the rest of the staff at Lucky 13 Book Reviews and News —thank you for all your help!

To my beta readers—Allena, Ame, Angi, Cathy, Charla, Debbie, Elizabeth, Felisha, Jen, Joanne, Katie, Milynn, Olivia, Rhonda, Susan, and Tawnya— you all are AWESOME! And thanks to Susan, Carrie, and KD for double checking my Delta Force facts! *smooches*

To the Sexy Six-Pack's Sirens group—as always, your continued support means more to me than you'll ever know! I love interacting with you and wish we could all meet someday in one place—what a party that would be!

To my readers—I hope you enjoyed Frisco and Haven's story. It is because of all of you that I keep telling the stories flying through my mind.

To Jess, Jules, Brandie, and Kelle—Your continued support and friendship are things I will always cherish. While I was writing this book, we went through some ups and downs with health issues and other problems, but thank goodness we're still together (and Z. got what he needed).

The story within these pages is completely fictional but the concepts of BDSM are real. If you do choose to participate in the BDSM lifestyle, please research it carefully and take all precautions to protect yourself. Fiction is based on real life but real life is not based on fiction. Remember—Safe, Sane and Consensual!

Any information regarding persons or places has been used with creative literary license so there may be discrepancies between fiction and reality. The Navy SEALs' and Delta Force operatives' missions and personal qualities within have been created to enhance the story and, again, may be exaggerated and not coincide with reality.

The author has full respect for the members of the United States military and the varied members of law enforcement and thanks them for their continuing service to making this country as safe and free as possible.

ABOUT THE AUTHOR

A proud member of Romance Writers of America (RWA), Samantha A. Cole is a retired policewoman and former paramedic who is thrilled to add award-winning author to her list of exciting careers. She has lived her entire life in the suburbs of New York City and is looking forward to becoming a snow-bird between New York and Florida someday. Her two fur-babies, Jinx and Bella, keep her company and remind their mom to take a break from writing every once in a while to go for a walk, which is the best way to deal with a stubborn case of writer's block.

An avid reader since childhood, Samantha was often found with a book in hand and sometimes one in each. After being gifted with a stack of romance novels from her grandmother, her love affair with the genre began in her teens. Many years later, she discovered her love for writing stories was just as strong. Taking her life experiences and training, she strives to find the perfect mix of suspense and romance for her readers to enjoy.

Her standalone novel, The Friar, won the silver medal in the 2017 Readers' Favorite Awards in the Contemporary Romance genre out of more than 1000 entries.

While the original planned stories for the Trident Security series have been completed, they have brought many opportunities for Samantha to spread her wings and bring her readers more characters and stories to love. Look for her new Trident Security Omega Team series, Doms of The Covenant Novella series, Blackhawk Security series, and more from the Malone Brothers series, in addition to several standalone projects.

<u>Sexy Six-Pack's Sirens Group on Facebook</u>
<u>Website</u>
<u>Subscribe to my newsletter</u>
<u>All Author</u>

Facebook
—www.facebook.com/SamanthaColeAuthor/

Twitter—www.twitter.com/SamanthaCole222

Amazon—www.amazon.com/Samantha-A.-
Cole/e/B00X53K3X8

Book Bub—www.smarturl.it/SACbookbub

Youtube—www.smarturl.it/SamanthaColeYoutube

Instagram
—www.instagram.com/samanthacoleauthor/

Pinterest—www.pinterest.com/samanthacoleaut/

Goodreads—www.smarturl.it/SACGR

Fire and Police: Operation Alpha World

As you know, this book included at least one character from Susan Stoker's books. To check out more, see below.

Delta Force Heroes Series

Rescuing Rayne (FREE!)

Rescuing Aimee (novella)

Rescuing Emily

Rescuing Harley

Marrying Emily

Rescuing Kassie

Rescuing Bryn

Rescuing Casey

Rescuing Sadie

Rescuing Wendy

Rescuing Mary (Oct 2018)

Rescuing Macie (April 2019)

Badge of Honor: Texas Heroes Series

Justice for Mackenzie (FREE!)

Justice for Mickie

Justice for Corrie

Justice for Laine (novella)

Shelter for Elizabeth

Justice for Boone

Shelter for Adeline

Shelter for Sophie

Justice for Erin

Justice for Milena

Shelter for Blythe

Justice for Hope (Sept 2018)

Shelter for Quinn (Feb 2019)

Shelter for Koren (June 2019)

Shelter for Penelope (Oct 2019)

SEAL of Protection Series

Protecting Caroline (FREE!)

Protecting Alabama

Protecting Fiona

Marrying Caroline (novella)

Protecting Summer

Protecting Cheyenne

Protecting Jessyka

Protecting Julie (novella)

Protecting Melody

Protecting the Future

Protecting Kiera (novella)

Protecting Dakota

SEAL of Protection: Legacy Series

Securing Caite (Jan 2019)

Securing Sidney (May 2019)
Securing Piper (Sept 2019)
Securing Zoey (TBA)
Securing Avery (TBA)
Securing Kalee (TBA)

New York Times, *USA Today* and *Wall Street Journal* Bestselling Author Susan Stoker has a heart as big as the state of Texas where she lives, but this all American girl has also spent the last fourteen years living in Missouri, California, Colorado, and Indiana. She's married to a retired Army man who now gets to follow *her* around the country.

She debuted her first series in 2014 and quickly followed that up with the SEAL of Protection Series, which solidified her love of writing and creating stories readers can get lost in.

If you enjoyed this book, or any book, please consider leaving a review. It's appreciated by authors more than you'll know.

www.stokeraces.com

www.AcesPress.com

susan@stokeraces.com

36005953R00156

Made in the USA
Middletown, DE
15 February 2019